Lint, Socks and Rock Paper Scissors

Strange Competitions: Where Passion Meets Absurdity

Henri Penuer

Two Hungry Bowlers Publishing

Two Hungry Bowlers Publishing

30 N Gould Street Suite N

Sheridan, WY 82801

FIRST EDITION

ISBN: 979-8-9922799-0-0

Library of Congress Control Number: 2025900352

Four decades ago, I found my best friend.

Since then, I've been blessed to also call her my wife.

Acknowledgements

To Laura, Mark, Kathryn and Robyn - my fearless beta readers who ventured into early drafts and emerged with invaluable insights. Your thoughtful feedback helped shape these peculiar tales into something coherent.

Henri

Isn't the ability to find complexity in simplicity, to create meaning where none existed before, one of our species' most remarkable traits? And if that means spending decades studying the metaphysical implications of belly button lint or the secret language of ceiling fans, well, perhaps that's exactly what makes us human.

Contents

Introduction 1

The Existential Crisis of Garden Gnomes 5

Decoding the Language of Ceiling Fans 9

The Secret Life of Rubber Ducks 13

The Fascinating World of Dust Bunnies 19

Refrigerator Rendezvous: A Study of Magnetic Personalities 23

The Twisted Path to Knowledge 27

Analysis of Rock, Paper, Scissors Dynamics 31

Decoding the Mysteries of Belly Button Lint 35

The Art of Sniffing and Appreciating Everyday Odors 39

The Fascinating World of Lost Hair Scrunchies 43

Decoding the Language of Shoes Laces 47

Chopstick Juggling 53

The Lost Art of Paper Clip Sculpting 57

The Napkin Whisperer 61

Competitive Pencil Sharpening 67

The Great Pillow Schism: A Tale of Two Leagues 71

Extreme Competitive Eyebrow Dancing 77

Mastering the Art of Competitive Staring 81

The Exit 47 Method: Bubble Wrap Popping 85

Extreme Thumb Wrestling 89

When Puzzle Pieces Vanish 93

Competitive Yodeling for Beginners 99

Lost Socks: Where Do They Go 103

Mastering the Art of Competitive Yawning 107

Ending Thoughts - The Science of Taking Things Too Se- 111
riously

Appendice 115

Research Notes from the Reject Pile: A Peer-Reviewed 117
Collection of Misfit Studies

Extreme Sock Folding 119

Mastering the Art of Competitive Kazoo Playing 123

Competitive Rubber Band Archery (Draft for submission) 127

Afterword 130

Introduction

Introduction

As I sit here in my office at the International Institute of Improbable Research, surrounded by three decades' worth of meticulously cataloged documentation of humanity's most overlooked achievements in overthinking, I can't help but marvel at how far our field has come. We are living, I dare say, in the golden age of taking silly things seriously. From the metaphysical implications of belly button lint to the precise art of competitive eyebrow dancing, our research has spanned the full spectrum of human obsession with the trivial.

Throughout my years of research, I've had the privilege of observing and categorizing three distinct schools of unnecessary studies: the Meticulous Observers (Academicus obsessivus), the Data-Driven Documentarians (Academicus statisticus), and the more controversial Theoretical Overthinkists (Academicus excessivus). Each group brings its own unique methodologies and philosophies to our shared pursuit of studying the absolutely ordinary.

One of my most esteemed colleagues, Dr. Penny Fuzz-Worth, exemplifies the dedication required in our field. I'll never forget watching her adjust her custom-designed microscope for optimal dust bunny observation while telling me, "People think we're just making this up." She wasn't, of course. At that level of analysis, one is truly exploring the profound implications of everyday absurdity.

The evolution of our equipment has been fascinating to witness. What began as simple tools has grown into an impressive array of specialized instruments. Our Basic Research Kit now includes calibrated overthinking tools, significance detectors, and what we affectionately call our "reality check station" – essential equipment for maintaining optimal academic pretension. I've seen many colleagues upgrade to controversial equipment like the "Importance Inflator 3000" and climate-controlled ego chambers, though I maintain a healthy skepticism about such advanced apparatus.

My colleague Dr. Heinrich von Seriouss's work in identifying personality types among our practitioners has been invaluable. I've encountered countless "Dedicated Documentarians" who approach each topic as if it were the key to solving world hunger, and numerous "Passionate Pedants" who find their calling in counting things nobody needs counted. I must admit, I see a bit of both types in myself. There's also the "Theoretical Overthinkists," who can spend years pondering the philosophical implications of a single dust bunny.

But perhaps what brings me the most joy is documenting the extraordinary world of hobbyists who have elevated their passions into art forms. From the breathtaking precision of champion competitive thumb wrestlers to the Zen-like focus of master competitive yawners, these dedicated individuals remind us that the pursuit of meaning knows no bounds. Their commitment to mastering the utterly unnecessary serves as a testament to the human spirit's endless capacity for finding significance in the seemingly insignificant.

What I've learned through my years of study is that true understanding lies not in finding meaning, but in creating it where none existed before. Whether we're examining the metaphysical implications of navel lint or documenting the regional variations in competitive shoelace tying, we're really exploring the boundless creativity of the human spirit.

Some might question the value of studying such seemingly trivial matters with such intensity. To them, I say: look closer. In every carefully documented dust bunny, in every precisely measured belly button cavity, in every meticulously recorded yodeling competition, we find something profound about human nature – our remarkable capacity to find passion, meaning, and community in the most unexpected places.

As I continue my work here at the IIIR, I remain committed to shining a light on these overlooked corners of human endeavor. For in these seemingly insignificant pursuits, we find the true measure of human creativity and dedication. After all, isn't the ability to take something ordinary and imbue it with extraordinary meaning one of humanity's most remarkable traits?

Now, if you'll excuse me, I believe Dr. Marjorie Threadwell has made a breakthrough in the field of lint migration patterns, and I simply must document it for posterity.

Dr. Henri Penuer

12th December

Ashton Croft, On the Mend,

England

The Existential Crisis of Garden Gnomes

Lecture Hall B was unusually crowded that autumn morning. Professor Margaret Gardenthought's course, "Introduction to Ornamental Metaphysics 101," had gained quite a reputation across campus. Today's topic: the philosophical awakening of garden gnomes.

"Ladies and gentlemen," Professor Gardenthought began, adjusting the focus on her presentation slide showing a particularly contemplative gnome, "what we're witnessing in suburban gardens across America is nothing short of a philosophical revolution."

A student's hand shot up. "Professor, are you suggesting that garden gnomes... think?"

"Think?" Professor Gardenthought's eyes gleamed with academic fervor. "Young man, they don't merely think — they philosophize! Consider Specimen 472, whom we've named Socrates." She gestured to a weathered fishing gnome perched on her lecture podium. "Note how his eternal pursuit of an uncatchable fish mirrors our own quest for unattainable knowledge."

The students scribbled frantically as she outlined her groundbreaking theory of gnome consciousness development. According to her research, each gnome went through distinct philosophical stages: from naive garden decoration to enlightened lawn sage.

"Here we see the transformation," she continued, clicking through slides of gradually weathering gnomes. "The 'Wheelbarrow Crisis' typically occurs around year three, when the gnome begins questioning the purpose of eternally pushing an empty load. This often leads to what we term the 'Great Gardening Existential Breakthrough.'"

During weekly field observations, her graduate students documented fascinating behavioral patterns. The notorious "Midnight Migrations" the tendency of gnomes to be found in slightly different positions each morning had sparked heated debate in academic circles.

"Our time-lapse cameras have captured something extraordinary," Professor Gardenthought announced, playing a grainy video. "What appears to be a weekly philosophical discussion group, led by elderly Mushroom Sitters the acknowledged sages of garden society."

The department's annual Garden Consciousness Conference had become legendary. Scholars arrived from around the world, each bringing their most philosophically advanced specimens. The heated debate between the Orthodox Concrete Traditionalists and the Progressive Resin Reformers had nearly ended in a fistfight last year.

Professor Gardenthought's own contribution to the field, "The Epistemology of Lawn Ornamentation," had revolutionized the way academics viewed garden decorations. Her controversial thesis suggested that pink flamingos served as devil's advocates in garden philosophical discourse, deliberately challenging gnome conventional wisdom.

"Consider the implications," she would tell her wide-eyed students. "Every garden is a potential philosophical salon. Those aren't decorative mushrooms they're sitting on they're contemplation platforms!"

Her research methods raised eyebrows even among her most supportive colleagues. The installation of tiny philosophical texts in miniature waterproof libraries throughout test gardens had been particularly controversial. "But how else," she argued, "can we test their reading preferences? The Nietzsche volumes consistently show more weathering than the Plato."

The university administration remained skeptical, especially after the incident with the meditation chimes and the neighbors' noise complaints. But student enrollment in Ornamental Metaphysics courses had tripled since Professor Gardenthought's arrival.

Her graduate students learned to cope with her eccentricities. The requirement to address each research gnome by its philosophical honorific ("Doctor" or "Professor") had seemed strange at first, but now felt perfectly natural. The weekly garden philosophy workshops, where students sat silently with their assigned gnomes, had a surprisingly calming effect on academic stress levels.

As the semester progressed, even the most skeptical students found themselves pausing thoughtfully before garden displays. "You see it now, don't you?" Professor Gardenthought would ask, noting their growing awareness. "Behind those painted smiles lies an entire universe of philosophical inquiry."

And so, lecture by lecture, paper by paper, Professor Gardenthought built her academic legacy. Her latest project, a comprehensive translation of what she termed "gnome wisdom literature," interpreted through erosion patterns and lichen growth, promised to revolutionize the field once again.

As she told each incoming class, "In the great garden of knowledge, every gnome is a seed of wisdom. We need only learn to listen to their silent teachings."

The mushroom-sitting gnome on her desk nodded imperceptibly in agreement. Or perhaps it was just the air conditioning.

Decoding the Language of Ceiling Fans

The ceiling fan in the living room had always been there, spinning lazily above, a guardian angel of coolness. But for Professor Eloise Brindle, it was more than just a household appliance. It was a mystery. And mysteries, as we all know, demand thorough investigation. So, Eloise embarked on an ethnographic study unlike any other: decoding the language of ceiling fans.

"What do you mean you're studying the fan, Mom?" her daughter, Becca, asked, one eyebrow arched in concern. "Not just studying, dear," Eloise replied, adjusting her reading glasses as she squinted at the oscillating blades. "I'm learning its language. It's clearly trying to communicate with us. You just need to listen closely."

Becca sighed and retreated to her room. Eloise was unfazed. She had already made progress. She'd determined that the fan had three distinct "dialects," corresponding to the three speed settings. Slow speed—"Lazy Whisper"—spoke in soft murmurs, a language she suspected was reserved for soothing pets and lulling insomniacs to sleep. Medium speed—"Mild Panic"—was the language of family arguments, the kind of setting you'd use to match the tension when someone spilled spaghetti sauce on the new rug. And high speed—"Cyclonic Rage"—was a fierce declaration, used mostly during July heatwaves and teenage tantrums.

Eloise had documented all these findings in her notebook, now titled "The Fan Speaks: A Linguistic Journey". The real breakthrough came one rainy afternoon when she noticed the fan would make different noises depending on who was in the room. When Becca entered, the fan made a soft clicking sound, almost like a nervous teenager cracking their knuckles. But when her husband, Frank, plodded in, the fan gave off a low, groaning rattle—the equivalent, Eloise suspected, of an exasperated eye roll.

Eloise became certain that the fan was a keen observer of human behavior. She took to testing this theory, turning the fan on during different scenarios. When she turned it on during Frank's recounting of his golf game for the third time that week, the fan's chain began to swing violently, almost like it was trying to say, "Enough, Frank! Let it go!" Eloise took this as confirmation: the fan was not only sentient, but also a rather discerning critic.

Her next step was to communicate back. Eloise began to use the wall switch in Morse code. Flick-flick-pause-flick. "Hello, Ceiling Fan," she tapped out one evening. She waited. The fan responded with a wobble and a light squeak. Eloise's eyes widened.

She tried again. Flick-flick-flick. "How are you?"

The fan, after a moment's contemplation, responded with a slow creak, followed by a gentle rattle. Eloise was thrilled. "I think it's saying 'tired,'" she murmured, scribbling frantically into her notebook.

By now, the rest of the family was growing more concerned. "Is Mom... talking to the fan?" Becca whispered to her dad one evening, as Eloise held up a hand to shush them, her eyes fixed on the whirling blades. Frank sighed deeply, glancing at the TV remote longingly. "Let her be, sweetheart. I think she's happy," he said.

But it wasn't until Eloise hosted a neighborhood gathering—Ceiling Fan Cultural Appreciation Night—that things truly escalated. She invited over the neighbors, laid out cheese platters, and positioned chairs in a circle under the fan, as though they were preparing for some cultish meeting. Everyone sat awkwardly, while Eloise began her presentation, detailing how their ceiling fan was a wise and discerning household entity.

"Watch as it observes," she said, as she clicked the fan on to speed two. The crowd stared up in silence. The fan, sensing the audience, gave a slow, mysterious wobble, which Eloise interpreted as a greeting. She was ecstatic.

The neighbors, however, weren't convinced. Mrs. Jenkins, who lived next door, leaned over to Becca and whispered, "Is your mother okay, dear?"

Becca sighed. "She's just... passionate about air circulation." She paused, then added, "And maybe she has a point. It does seem a little sassier when Dad's around."

The evening culminated with Eloise offering "fan readings," where attendees could stand under the fan while she interpreted the noises it made. Mrs. Jenkins received a "soft thrum," which Eloise said indicated a promising week ahead, while Mr. Thompson's "sharp rattle" meant he should probably check his cholesterol. Frank refused to participate, retreating to the back of the room where he quietly nibbled on crackers, muttering something about needing to find a new hobby.

As the guests departed, each slightly bewildered, Eloise turned to the fan and flicked the wall switch three times—her way of saying "Thank you." The fan gave a gentle sway, and Eloise smiled. "You're welcome," she whispered back.

And so, Professor Eloise Brindle concluded her first major ethnographic study. Her conclusion? Not only do ceiling fans have personalities, but they also possess a certain wisdom, one that can only be understood by those willing to listen. She couldn't wait for her next study—The Existential Cries of the Toaster.

Becca, for her part, just hoped this one wouldn't involve inviting the neighbors.

The Secret Life of Rubber Ducks

Field Notes on the Migratory Patterns of Domestic Anatidae:

A Scientific Investigation into the Secret Lives of Rubber Ducks

    Department of Synthetic Wildlife Studies

    Institute for Domestic Object Migration

    Date: 12/18/24

    Field Report 247

    Principal Investigator: Dr. Eleanor Quackworth

Day 147 of observation: Another remarkable breakthrough in our understanding of rubber duck migration patterns. After installing our state-of-the-art PlumbTrack™ sensors throughout the city's drainage system, we've documented what appears to be a coordinated movement of approximately 347 specimens, all heading toward what we theorize to be their seasonal gathering point.

The specimens demonstrate fascinating behavioral patterns previously unknown to science. Using our Aquatic Resonance Detection Equipment (ARDE), we've recorded complex sequences of squeaks that suggest a sophisticated form of communication. Dr. Martinez from the Synthetic Vocalization Lab suggests these may be migration calls, though Dr. Wong maintains they're merely the result of water pressure variations. The debate continues to rage in academic circles.

Specimen 21, nicknamed "Admiral Yellow" due to its unusually authoritative squeak, has proven particularly intriguing. Through careful tracking, we've observed it leading groups of younger ducks through complex pipe networks, teaching what appears to be advanced navigation techniques. The precision with which these maneuvers are executed suggests a level of organizational hierarchy previously unthought possible in synthetic waterfowl.

Our latest funding proposal to the National Institute of Bathroom Studies (NIBS) has been met with some skepticism. "While Dr. Quackworth's research is... unique," wrote Dr. Harriet Tubsworth in her review, "the suggestion that rubber ducks maintain an underground society complete with educational systems and governmental structures seems, perhaps, ambitious." She clearly hasn't seen our infrared footage of the midnight rubber duck parliament.

The discovery of what we've termed "duck highways" - preferred migration routes through the city's plumbing infrastructure - has revolutionized our understanding of synthetic waterfowl behavior. These routes, marked by subtle scratch patterns on pipe surfaces, suggest decades of established migration patterns. Carbon dating of the scratch marks indicates some routes may predate indoor plumbing itself, raising fascinating questions about rubber duck evolution.

Critical to our research has been the development of the Mini-Submersible Duck Tracking Unit (MSDTU), a microscopic camera system designed to follow migrating specimens. The footage obtained has been nothing short of revolutionary, though we lost three research assistants to what they described as "the existential horror of discovering where the ducks actually go." Their letters of resignation were unusually damp.

Of particular interest is the ducks' apparent ability to materialize in impossible locations. We've documented appearances in sealed coffee thermoses, locked briefcases, and once, memorably, inside the International Space Station. NASA continues to deny our requests for a joint research project, though the astronauts' reports of squeaking sounds during orbital night phases support our theories.

The seasonal gathering phenomenon, which we've termed the "Great Convergence," remains our most puzzling observation. Every third full moon, thousands of specimens gather in what we believe to be vast underground caverns. Our only footage of these gatherings is extremely limited, as our equipment tends to malfunction in the presence of large rubber duck assemblies. The one clear image we obtained shows what appears to be a ritual dance around a giant, possibly golden, duck statue. The peer review board has suggested this might be a lens flare. They are wrong.

Future research will focus on decoding the complex system of bath toy hierarchies we've observed. Preliminary data suggests rubber ducks maintain diplomatic relations with other bath toys, though tensions with rubber frogs remain high for reasons unknown.

Funding Update: The Institute has approved our request for an expanded research facility, though they've asked us to explain the line item "emergency rubber duck containment unit" in more detail. They clearly don't remember the Great Duck Uprising of 2023.

A Note on Safety: All field researchers are reminded to maintain proper distance from specimens displaying unusual color variations or excessive squeaking. The incident with the glow-in-the-dark duck that predicted stock market crashes remains under investigation.

Next Quarter's Goals:

- Complete construction of the deep-pipe monitoring network

- Decode the mysterious "song of the ducks" recorded during full moons

- Determine why rubber ducks seem to multiply when not directly observed

- Investigate reports of duck-led resistance movements in premium spa facilities

The mystery of rubber duck migration continues to deepen with each new discovery. As we prepare for next month's expedition into the city's main drainage system, I can't help but wonder: are we studying the ducks, or are they studying us?

Note: This report was typed by my research assistant, as my own keyboard is currently occupied by a small colony of rubber ducks that refuse to leave and have begun organizing what appears to be a labor union.

Dr. Eleanor Quackworth

Principal Investigator

Department of Synthetic Wildlife Studies

P.S.

•

: If anyone finds my car keys, please return them. A duck took them three days ago; and I've been sleeping in the lab since.

The Fascinating World of Dust Bunnies

You know those fuzzy little balls of fluff you find under your couch? Well, let me tell you about Dr. Penny Dust-Worth – she's spent thirty years studying them. No, really! She's basically the Jane Goodall of dust bunnies, except instead of hanging out in the jungle, she's crawling around under people's furniture with a flashlight and a really expensive camera.

"But they're just dust!" I hear you say. Oh boy, are you in for a treat. According to Dr. Dust-Worth, there's this whole hidden world under your bed that's better organized than your sock drawer.

Here's the thing: dust bunnies come in three flavors. You've got your everyday corner dwellers – the ones playing hide and seek behind your TV stand. Then there's these weird floating ones that seem to defy gravity – they're like the astronauts of the dust world. But the real celebrities? Those massive dust monsters under your bed. You know, the ones that might actually be holding onto that sock you lost three years ago.

I met this fascinating researcher, Martha Sweepington (I swear, these names!), who spends her days mapping dust bunny territories like some kind of indoor explorer. She showed me her work diary, and let me tell you, it reads like a nature documentary script. "Day 47: The large specimen under the chaise lounge has absorbed a pencil eraser. Fascinating."

And get this – they've got actual tools for studying these things. Not just your regular magnifying glass and tweezers, oh no. We're talking about high-tech "dust preservation chambers" (fancy boxes) and something called a "Particle Pattern Predictor" (which I'm pretty sure is just a really expensive way to guess where the next dust bunny will pop up).

The really wild part? Location matters! Dust bunnies in Arizona are like the desert survivalists of the dust world – tough, dry, and ready for anything. Meanwhile, Norwegian dust bunnies are basically the Vikings of the dust realm, built to handle long, dark winters under Nordic furniture.

There's this one researcher, Dr. von Staubheimer (honestly, where do they find these people?), who's written an entire book about dust. He's identified different dust bunny personalities – you've got your quick growers in busy areas and your slow-and-steady types that hide in corners plotting world domination or something.

And here's the kicker — this is actually big business! Vacuum companies are throwing millions at dust bunny research. I guess knowing your enemy is half the battle, right? Though there's this one guy, Vladimir Dustanov, who's basically the dust bunny whisperer, who says all you need is a flashlight and patience. He holds the record for finding the biggest under-bed dust bunny, which I imagine is like winning an Olympic medal in the dust research world.

But wait, there's more! The scientific community was rocked last year when Dr. Dust-Worth published her groundbreaking paper, "Social Networks in Domestic Dust Accumulations: A Ten-Year Study." Turns out, dust bunnies aren't the loners we thought they were. They form complex communities, with smaller dust bunnies often clustering around a larger, more established one – like tiny dust suburbs around a dust metropolis.

The history of dust bunny research is equally fascinating. In the 1950s, Dr. Margaret Dustfield conducted the first formal study using what she called her "wait and watch" methodology, which basically meant sitting very still in people's living rooms for hours. Her pioneering work laid the foundation for modern dust dynamics, though her colleagues thought she was just napping on the job.

The economic impact is nothing to sneeze at either. Besides vacuum companies, there's now a whole industry built around "dust management solutions." We're talking specialized filters, air quality monitors, and even dust bunny forecasting services. There's even a startup in Silicon Valley working on AI-powered dust tracking (though personally, I think they're just blowing smoke).

And let's not forget the annual International Dust Bunny Symposium (IDBS), where researchers gather to share their findings. Last year's hot topic? The controversial "Five-Second Rule" as it applies to dust bunny formation. Dr. Helmut Fuzzheimer's presentation "Speed Dating: Rapid Dust Accumulation Patterns" had everyone on the edge of their seats – or under them, looking for samples.

Dr. Dust-Worth has this great saying: "True understanding lies not in what we clean away, but in what we learn before we do." Which is either profound wisdom or just a really good excuse not to vacuum.

So next time you're cleaning under your furniture and find a dust bunny, remember; you're not just looking at dirt – you're looking at what might be the next breakthrough in domestic debris science. Just don't tell Dr. Dust-Worth where you found it, or she might show up with her research team and camp out under your couch.

Refrigerator Rendezvous: A Study of Magnetic Personalities

In my dimly lit kitchen at 2 AM, where the gentle hum of my refrigerator provides the soundtrack to another late-night magnet cataloging session, I find myself chatting with Sandra, my fellow magnet enthusiast from Perth, Australia. "You won't believe what I found at the estate sale today," I type, carefully photographing my latest acquisition - a rare 1957 Disneyland promotional magnet featuring Mickey Mouse with unusual ferrite composition.

The taxonomy of refrigerator magnets has become our shared obsession. Sandra and I have identified five distinct categories through our years of virtual collaboration: the Tourist Trophy Collection (Magneticus souveniris), the Functional Document Holders (Magneticus practicus), the Handcrafted Artisanal Series (Magneticus aestheticus), the Nostalgic Novelty Group (Magneticus nostalgicus), and our personal favorite, the Rare Vintage Specimens (Magneticus antiquus).

"The patina on this one is remarkable," I message Sandra, adjusting my desk lamp for better illumination. "The oxidation pattern suggests it spent decades on a Frigidaire." Sandra responds with her own late-night discovery - a pristine set of magnetic fruit from a 1960s kitchen catalog she found in a thrift store.

My apartment has become what I jokingly call the "Institute of Domestic Magnetism," though it's really just my kitchen with specialized equipment carefully arranged around my coffee maker. The Basic Analysis Kit (a birthday gift from Sandra) includes a gauss meter, surface tension calculator, and what we call our "memory matrix" – a shared digital database for mapping our combined collections.

"Remember that theory we had about the migration patterns of tourist magnets?" I type to Sandra, examining a curious cluster forming on my fridge door. "I'm seeing it again - the Vegas ones keep gravitating toward the Atlantic City group." Sandra sends back a laughing emoji, followed by a photo of her own geographically organized collection.

Our late-night sessions often involve detailed discussions about preservation techniques. My homemade humidity-controlled display case (constructed from a modified clear storage bin) houses the most delicate specimens. Sandra has been experimenting with different coating techniques for her outdoor-displayed pieces, sharing her successes and failures in our nightly chats.

"Do you ever think we're taking this too seriously?" I ask Sandra around 3 AM, as I adjust the position of a particularly stubborn magnetic letters set from 1973. Her response comes quickly: "Says the woman who installed a magnetic field meter in her kitchen."

We've developed our own shorthand for describing our finds. "Got a T3-N2 today," I message, our code for a third-generation tourist magnet with level 2 nostalgia factor. Sandra responds with photos of her latest "V5-R1" - a fifth-generation vintage piece with rare variant design.

The digital world has transformed our hobby. Through our iPads, we've created a virtual community of serious collectors, though few match our level of dedication. "Did you see the new collector in the forum trying to pass off a reproduction as original?" Sandra messages, adding an eye-roll emoji. "Amateur hour - didn't even check the ferrite composition."

I remember my first serious piece - a promotional magnet from the 1962 Seattle World's Fair that I found in my grandmother's kitchen drawer. The moment I held that space-age design, with its retro-futuristic Space Needle reaching toward painted stars, I was hooked. Sandra's origin story is equally serendipitous; she inherited a collection of vintage Australian tourist magnets from her great-aunt, each one a tiny time capsule of mid-century travel.

Our shared fascination with magnetic fields extends beyond mere collecting. We've documented the subtle ways different refrigerator surfaces affect magnetic strength, and I've mapped out what we call "sweet spots" - areas on my fridge where the magnetic hold seems mysteriously stronger. Sandra has developed a theory about how the earth's magnetic field might influence these patterns, though we both admit it might be our imagination running wild at 3 AM.

The gentle click-clack of magnets being rearranged has become my midnight meditation. Each piece has its own distinctive sound - the hollow plastic snap of tourist magnets, the solid thunk of vintage metal ones, the soft shuffle of flexible advertising pieces. Sandra and I have even discussed creating a sound library of these acoustic signatures, another layer of documentation in our ever-expanding research.

As another night of cataloging draws to a close, I send Sandra one final message: "In life, as in magnet collecting, it's not about what sticks to our fridges, but the connections we make along the way." She responds with a photo of her sunrise - as my night ends, her day of magnet hunting is just beginning.

The Twisted Path to Knowledge

Professor Mark "twisty" Soho's laboratory hummed with the sound of precision torque meters. His research team, a dedicated group of closure scientists, huddled around their latest discovery: a twist tie that had maintained optimal bread freshness for an unprecedented forty-seven days.

"Fascinating," Mark murmured, adjusting his specialized twist-analysis goggles. "The molecular alignment is unlike anything we've seen before." His graduate student, Chuck Toast, frantically documented every observation while trying to hide the sandwich in his lab coat—its store-bought clip closure would have been considered heresy in these hallowed halls.

The Department of Closure Studies occupied a peculiar place within the Institute of Packaging Sciences. Their wing was easily identifiable by the wall-to-wall display cases of historically significant twist ties, each authenticated and dated. "That's from the Great Bread Revolution of 1983," Mark would tell visitors, pointing to a particularly weathered specimen. "The day bakers realized that proper closure technique could extend shelf life by 43%."

The department's equipment room resembled a cross between a physics lab and a bakery. Precision torque meters hummed alongside specialized preservation chambers, while the controversial Molecular Stress Analyzer (still pending ethics approval) dominated the corner. Mark had once joked that they had enough humidity-controlled testing environments to supply a tropical greenhouse.

Through years of research, Mark and his team had identified distinct schools of twist methodology. Their classification system, developed through the infamous "Thousand Twists" study, had pushed several graduate students to the brink of carpal tunnel syndrome. After that, the study was baked into the archives, never to be seen again. But it was their groundbreaking paper on the "Quantum Preservation Theory" that truly shook the academic world. The theory suggested that certain twist patterns could create localized time dilation effects, essentially freezing the bread's aging process.

"Professor," Chuck interrupted Mark's contemplation. "Your son Colin called. He wants to know if you're coming home for dinner or if you're still trying to prove that twist ties can bend space-time."

"Tell him the space-time research is on hold," Mark replied, not looking up from his microscope. "We've discovered something far more intriguing—evidence of twist tie migration patterns between different kitchen drawers."

The laboratory's monthly research presentation always drew a crowd. Scholars from various departments would gather to witness Mark's latest findings, though many suspected they came for the perfectly preserved baked goods more than the science. Today's topic: "The Socioeconomic Impact of Improper Twist Technique on Global Bread Markets."

"Notice," Mark demonstrated, projecting a complex graph, "how regions with poor twist discipline show a 23% increase in bread-related disappointment." His research assistant, Dr. James "Tiedye" Thompson, nodded sagely while discretely untangling a particularly stubborn specimen. Thompson's signature "Double Helix Lock" technique had become legendary in closure science circles, though some questioned his claim of being able to achieve it blindfolded.

The department's annual budget meetings were legendary. Mark would arrive with mountains of data, fresh bread samples, and, occasionally, interpretive dancers to demonstrate optimal twist patterns. The dean had learned to schedule these meetings before lunch—hunger made the board more receptive to proposals involving artisanal bread preservation techniques.

Their latest research project involved collaboration with the quantum physics department. "If we can understand how twist ties appear in places they weren't left," Mark explained to his team, "we might unlock the secrets of quantum entanglement." The physicists remained skeptical, but couldn't explain why their break room suddenly had better-preserved pastries.

At home, Mark's family had learned to adapt. His partner Ashton managed the household's "civilian" bread storage needs, while their son Marcus had become surprisingly popular at school trading perfectly preserved sandwiches. The family's kitchen drawer organization system had been published in three scientific journals.

The future of closure science looked bright. Mark's team was on the verge of a breakthrough in biodegradable twist tie technology, though early prototypes had the unfortunate tendency to decompose exactly one day before the bread went stale. Meanwhile, their work on "smart" twist ties that could text you when your bread needed attention had attracted significant industry attention.

As Mark often told his students, "In the vast tapestry of packaging science, every twist and turn brings us closer to understanding the universe itself." Then he would adjust his goggles and return to his eternal quest to prove that proper twist tie technique could, theoretically, solve world hunger.

The dean recently approved funding for her most ambitious project yet: a twist tie particle accelerator. The physics department was concerned, but the cafeteria staff had never been happier.

Analysis of Rock, Paper, Scissors Dynamics

Professor Victoria "Lightning Hands" Rockwell's laboratory buzzed with anticipation. Her research team at the Institute of Strategic Hand

Studies huddled around their latest breakthrough: a player who had achieved a statistically impossible seventeen consecutive victories using nothing but "rock."

"Extraordinary," Victoria murmured, adjusting her high-speed gesture-capture goggles. "The angular velocity of her wrist rotation completely defies conventional RPS theory." Her graduate student Tom "Scissors" Martinez frantically recorded data while hiding his bandaged thumb – an injury from yesterday's failed attempt at a new experimental throwing technique.

The Department of Rock-Paper-Scissors Dynamics occupied a contentious position within the Institute. Their wing was instantly recognizable by the wall-to-wall display cases of bronze-cast winning gestures, each captured at the exact moment of victory. "That's from the Great Tournament of 1997," Victoria would tell visitors, pointing to a particularly dramatic paper-beats-rock casting. "The day we discovered that left-handed players have a 0.03% advantage during solar eclipses."

Through decades of research, Victoria and her team had identified distinct throwing styles that challenged fundamental concepts of game theory. The "Avalanche Method" relied on psychological manipulation through repeated rock throws, while the "Floating Lotus" technique emphasized the elegant ambiguity of pre-throw finger positioning. But it was their groundbreaking paper on "Quantum Hand Superposition" that truly revolutionized the field, suggesting that a hand could exist in all three states simultaneously until observed by the opponent.

"Professor," Tom interrupted Victoria's contemplation of their latest slow-motion footage, "The Ethics Committee wants to know if your research into subliminal paper-suggesting techniques is still using voluntary subjects."

"Tell them the hypnosis experiments are on hold," Victoria replied, not looking up from her monitor. "We've discovered something far more intriguing – evidence of predictive hand positioning based on shoe choice."

The laboratory's weekly research presentations drew international attention. Scholars from various departments would gather to witness Victoria's latest findings, though many suspected they came more for the legendary post-presentation tournaments. Today's topic: "The Socioeconomic Impact of Rock Preference on Global Decision-Making."

"Notice," Victoria demonstrated, projecting a complex series of hand trajectories, "how regions with high rock usage show a 47% increase in decision-making gridlock." Her research assistant, Dr. James "The Boulder" Thompson, nodded sagely while nursing his third straight paper defeat of the morning.

The department's funding presentations were legendary. Victoria would arrive with mountains of statistical analyses, live demonstration teams, and occasionally, interpretive dancers to demonstrate optimal throwing rhythms. The dean had learned to schedule these meetings in rooms with circular tables – rectangular ones gave an unfair advantage to paper strategies.

Their latest research project involved collaboration with the quantum physics department. "If we can understand how players instinctively choose their next throw," Victoria explained to her team, "we might unlock the secrets of human consciousness itself." The physicists remained skeptical, but couldn't explain their losing streak in the inter-departmental tournament.

The training program for new researchers was notoriously intense. The infamous "Five Hundred Throws" initiation required students to perfect their technique against a mechanical opponent capable of analyzing micro-expressions. "By throw 250," Victoria would say, "you either develop pre-cognitive abilities or carpal tunnel syndrome."

Recent breakthroughs in their "Smart Glove" technology promised to revolutionize professional RPS competitions, though early prototypes had the unfortunate tendency to get stuck in scissor position during high-humidity conditions. Meanwhile, their work on AI-powered throw prediction had attracted significant attention from both the gaming industry and international negotiation teams.

As Victoria often told her students, "In the complex dance of hand-based decision-making, every throw brings us closer to understanding the fundamental nature of human choice." Then she would adjust her goggles and return to her eternal quest to prove that rock-paper-scissors could, theoretically, replace all forms of conflict resolution.

The university recently approved funding for her most ambitious project yet: a zero-gravity RPS arena. The physics department was baffled, but the astronaut training program had never been more interested.

Dr. Thompson still insists that his recent losing streak is part of a long-term strategic plan. The department's betting pool suggests otherwise.

Decoding the Mysteries of Belly Button Lint

In the hallowed halls of bodily observation studies, few topics have garnered such intense academic scrutiny as the phenomenon known colloquially as "belly button lint." For Professor Marjorie Threadwell, Distinguished Chair of Navel Studies at the prestigious Bodily Debris Institute, the pursuit of understanding this misunderstood substance has become more than mere research—it has become a calling.

"What do you mean you're studying belly button fluff, Mom?" her son Trevor asked, his face contorted in a mixture of confusion and second-hand embarrassment.

"Not studying, dear," Marjorie corrected, adjusting her specially-designed navel inspection goggles. "I'm documenting the complex sociological and material interactions occurring within the umbilical ecosystem." Trevor quietly backed away, making a mental note to tell his therapist about this latest development.

Through rigorous observation, Professor Threadwell has identified distinct classifications of lint formations that revolutionized the field. Her groundbreaking taxonomy, published in her landmark 2023 study, established three distinct categories: the Common Cotton Collector (Navellus ordinarius), the Synthetic Blend Accumulator (Navellus synthetica), and the rare and prestigious Merino Wool Formation (Navellus elegantus). "People think lint is just lint," she would often say, peering through her custom-designed lint microscope, "but each sample tells a story as unique as the navel that produced it."

Her research led her to Harold Pinkerton, a retired postal worker from Minnesota, whose legendary collection of personally harvested lint spans four decades. During their interviews, Marjorie meticulously documented his observations. "The winter specimens," he explained, adjusting his magnifying loupe, "tend toward the darker blues and grays, with a density you just don't see in summer collections." This revelation formed the basis for her seasonal variation theory, which suggested that wardrobe changes directly influence lint composition.

Among her most significant findings was the identification of Navellus elegantus, which occurs only in individuals who wear high-quality natural fibers. These specimens exhibit what she termed the "cashmere effect" – a delicate, almost cloudlike structure that maintains its form even under microscopic examination. "It's the difference between table wine and champagne," she would explain during her lectures at the Paris Museum of Personal Artifacts.

Her breakthrough came during what colleagues now refer to as "The Great Laundry Experiment of 2024." By meticulously documenting the relationship between fabric choice and lint production, Marjorie discovered what she terms the "Cotton Cascade Effect"—wherein certain textile combinations create what she describes as "perfect lint-forming conditions."

"Observe," she would say during department presentations, holding up a glass vial containing a particularly impressive specimen, "how the fibers intertwine in a counterclockwise pattern, suggesting the wearer favors left-handed shirt-buttoning techniques." Her colleagues would lean forward, squinting at the tiny gray ball with scholarly intensity.

The academic community's response has been mixed. Dr. Harold Puffington of the Institute for Microscopic Debris Studies called her work "groundbreaking," while others questioned the allocation of research funding to what they dismissively termed "navel-gazing." Marjorie remained undaunted, organizing the first International Symposium on Umbilical Deposits (ISUD).

The symposium, held in her living room due to what she termed "venue constraints," attracted a select group of equally dedicated researchers. Dr. Emily Fuzzworthy presented her controversial paper on the impact of seasonal wardrobes on lint coloration, while Professor James Bellybutton (no relation to the research subject) shared his findings on the correlation between lint density and personality types. Trevor, watching from the kitchen, whispered to his father, "Dad, should we be worried about Mom?" His father, George, sighed while pretending to take notes. "Your mother once spent six months studying the migration patterns of dust bunnies under the couch. This is actually quite tame in comparison."

The evening reached its climax with Marjorie's demonstration of her patented "Lint Extraction and Classification System" (LECS), a modified vacuum cleaner she swears can determine the thread count of the originating garment based on the acoustic properties of the suction process. As the symposium concluded, Marjorie was already planning her next project. "The dust patterns on ceiling fans show remarkable similarities to lint formation," she mused, eyes gleaming with academic fervor. "There might be a connection..." Trevor and George exchanged glances, silently agreeing to hide the stepladder.

And so, Professor Marjorie Threadwell continues her vital research, undeterred by skeptics and familial concerns alike. Her latest paper, "Correlations Between Navel Depth and Lint Accumulation Patterns: A Quantitative Analysis," is currently under peer review at the Journal of Improbable Research.

Trevor just hopes the next family dinner won't include lint sample collection.

The Art of Sniffing and Appreciating Everyday Odors

In the strange world of professional smell appreciation, where success is measured in nasal nuance and careers rise or fall on a single inhalation, Dr. Rosemary "The Nose" Whiffington stands as a towering figure. From her laboratory at the Institute of Quotidian Olfactory Studies (IQOS), she has spent three decades documenting what she calls "the invisible aromatic tapestry of everyday life."

The taxonomy of recreational sniffing reveals three distinct schools: the Urban Adventurists (Nasalis urbanis), the Domestic Bouquet Specialists (Nasalis domesticus), and the controversial Wild Scent Hunters (Nasalis naturalis). Each group maintains its own methodologies, rating systems, and deeply held beliefs about the true nature of olfactory appreciation.

Consider the case of Harold "Deep Breath" Peterson, legendary master of the Parking Garage School of scent appreciation. "People think underground parking is just exhaust and oil stains," he explains, demonstrating his signature three-phase sniffing technique. "But there's a story in every level – from the fresh concrete notes of P1 to the complex bacterial bouquet of P7."

The equipment requirements for serious sniffing have evolved considerably. The Basic Sniffing Kit, as recommended by the International Nose Society, includes a calibrated nostril dilator, scent-neutral clothing, and what practitioners call a "palette cleanser" – usually coffee beans or fresh lemon. Advanced sniffers often add specialized equipment like the controversial "Aroma Amplification Cone" and humidity-controlled nose masks.

Field research has revealed fascinating geographical variations in smell appreciation. The Montreal school emphasizes winter-specific scents, while Australian practitioners have developed techniques for detecting subtle variations in burnt toast. "Every region has its signature bouquet," notes Dr. Whiffington, "like a fingerprint made of molecules."

The social hierarchy within professional sniffing is precisely structured. Novices begin with simple categories like "Fresh Laundry" before advancing to more complex challenges such as "Three-Day-Old Office Refrigerator" or the prestigious "Mystery Storage Unit" division. Only after years of training can they attempt the legendary "Public Transit Challenge."

Dr. Heinrich von Schnozzle, author of "The Nose Knows: Memoirs of a Scent Hunter," has documented distinct sniffing styles among practitioners. "The 'Quick Flickers' use rapid, shallow inhalations," he observes, "while the 'Deep Dwellers' prefer sustained, meditative sniffs lasting up to thirty seconds."

The economic implications of professional sniffing cannot be ignored. Major corporations now employ certified nose consultants to evaluate "workplace aromatic ambiance." "Last year alone, we prevented three potential office relocations by identifying and neutralizing rogue microwave popcorn incidents," reveals Sarah Scentwell, CEO of Atmospheric Harmony Industries.

Environmental factors play a crucial role in sniffing success. The World Sniffing Championships maintain strict controls for temperature, humidity, and pollen count. "A single sneeze can destroy hours of careful olfactory preparation," explains Championship Director James Nostril.

Recent technological developments have sparked intense debate within the community. The introduction of electronic "super-sniffers" has traditionalists concerned about the future of their art. "If you need more than your own nose and dedication, you're missing the point," argues Vladimir Aromanov, holder of the current record for identifying breakfast cereals blindfolded.

Training regimens for professional sniffers border on the extreme. The legendary "Thousand Scents" exercise requires apprentices to identify one hundred different odors daily for ten days straight. "By day seven, most people can smell colors," notes Master Trainer Mai Wong. "By day nine, they're detecting wifi signals."

The psychological impact of intensive sniffing can be profound. Dr. Lisa Inhalton has documented what she terms "Post-Traumatic Scent Disorder" among retired professionals. "Some can never eat at food courts again," she notes. "The olfactory memories are too intense."

As interest in professional sniffing grows, concerns about performance enhancement have emerged. The World Anti-Doping Agency for Nasal Sports (WADANS) now tests for substances that might enhance olfactory sensitivity. "The integrity of the nose must match the integrity of the art," insists WADANS director Patricia Pungent.

For now, the elite world of professional sniffing continues to evolve, pushing the boundaries of human perception and patience. As Dr. Whiffington often remarks while calibrating her collection of vintage nose clips, "In life, as in sniffing, true mastery lies not in what you smell, but in how deeply you appreciate it."

The Fascinating World of Lost Hair Scrunchies

In the shadowy realm beneath couch cushions and behind washing machines, a peculiar phenomenon has long mystified domestic scientists and casual observers alike: the systematic disappearance of hair scrunchies.

These elastic-bound fabric circles, first popularized in the 1980s, have developed migratory patterns that would impress even the most seasoned naturalist.

Dr. Sarah McLaughlin, leading researcher in Domestic Object Migration Studies at the Institute of Household Mysteries, has spent fifteen years tracking the movement patterns of lost scrunchies. "What fascinates me," she notes, adjusting her own purple velvet scrunchie, "is how they seem to follow distinct disappearance routes that vary by household ecosystem."

The taxonomy of lost scrunchies reveals three primary species: the Bathroom Vanisher (Scrunchius evanescens), the Bedroom Wanderer (Scrunchius nomadicus), and the most elusive of all, the Car Console Dweller (Scrunchius automotivus). Each demonstrates unique behavioral patterns that have evolved to maximize their chances of escaping human detection.

Consider the case of the Henderson household in suburban Milwaukee. Martha Henderson, a high school teacher, documented the loss of 47 scrunchies over six months. "They were last seen on my bathroom counter," she recalls, her voice tinged with the resignation familiar to any scrunchie owner. "The next morning, nothing. Not even a thread left behind." Dr. McLaughlin's team later discovered a complex network of migration routes leading from the bathroom counter, through a small gap behind the vanity, and into what they term the "void zone" – a mysterious space where scrunchies seem to gather in numbers yet remain perpetually out of reach.

The Bedroom Wanderer presents an even more intriguing case study. Unlike its bathroom-dwelling cousin, this species exhibits a peculiar habit of appearing briefly in unexpected locations – under pillows, behind nightstands, tangled in curtain tassels – before vanishing again. Rebecca Liu, a graduate student working with Dr. McLaughlin, has proposed that these appearances might be territorial marking behaviors, though the scientific community remains divided on this interpretation.

Perhaps most remarkable is the Car Console Dweller, a hardy subspecies that has adapted to thrive in the harsh environment of automobile interiors. These scrunchies demonstrate an unprecedented ability to wedge themselves into seemingly impossible spaces, often reappearing months later in entirely different vehicles, suggesting a previously unknown form of scrunchie migration.

The economic impact of this phenomenon is not insignificant. The American Association of Hair Accessory Manufacturers estimates that the average household purchases replacement scrunchies at a rate of 3.7 times the actual need, directly attributable to unexplained losses. This translates to approximately $47 million in annual replacement costs nationwide.

Local scrunchie expert and vintage accessories dealer Mabel Thornton offers a more philosophical perspective. "Every lost scrunchie," she muses, running her fingers over her collection of rare 1990s specimens, "is really just finding its way home. We don't lose them – they choose to leave." Her words carry the weight of decades spent observing these mysterious accessories in their natural habitat.

Recent developments in tracking technology have allowed researchers to attach microscopic sensors to a sample group of scrunchies, though results have been inconclusive. The sensors invariably cease transmission within 48 hours of deployment, leading some scientists to speculate about the existence of scrunchie gathering points – locations beyond our current technological reach where these accessories congregate in numbers that defy imagination.

As our understanding of scrunchie behavior continues to evolve, one thing remains clear: these seemingly simple hair accessories harbor complexities that challenge our understanding of domestic object permanence.

Their disappearance patterns suggest an intelligence that raises uncomfortable questions about the nature of inanimate objects and their relationship to human organization systems.

For now, the mystery endures, marked only by the frustrated sighs of those searching for that perfect scrunchie that matched their favorite outfit – the one that was just here yesterday, its current location known only to whatever force governs the mysterious world of lost hair accessories.

Decoding the Language of Shoes Laces

From the Private Research Journals of Professor Beatrice Knotting-Wells

Director, Department of Aglet Studies
  Institute of Fastening Arts

September 15, 2024

Today marks my 3,427th consecutive day of shoelace observation. The specimens continue to reveal new secrets. This morning, I witnessed what can only be described as a spontaneous double-helix formation in Mr. Peterson's running shoes. He remained blissfully unaware of the mathematical miracle occurring at his feet.

September 16, 2024

Tom threatened to stage an "intervention" after finding my collection of historically significant aglets under his pillow. I tried explaining they needed to be kept at precise room temperature, but he seemed unreasonable. Emma suggested I needed a hobby. I reminded her that this IS my hobby. She suggested a different hobby.

September 20, 2024

BREAKTHROUGH! After months of painstaking research, I've successfully mapped the migration patterns of loose aglets across the average household. They appear to be drawn to washing machines, following what I've termed the "Sock Displacement Theory." Further study required.

October 1, 2024

Gave a guest lecture at the Annual Fastening Technologies Conference. My presentation on "The Socioeconomic Implications of Loop Length Variance" was well-received, though several colleagues appeared to develop sudden and inexplicable eye twitches during the three-hour demonstration.

October 15, 2024

Field observation has revealed a startling correlation between personality types and preferred lacing patterns:
- The "Over-Under Conformist": Follows rules, files taxes early
- The "Zigzag Rebel": Questions authority, probably has a secret tattoo
- The "Chaos Method": Either a genius or should not be allowed near shoes
Must publish findings immediately.

October 16, 2024

Emma caught me analyzing her shoelaces while she slept. In my defense, the pattern suggested possible career indecision. She's changed all her shoes to slip-ons in protest. Teenagers can be so dramatic.

October 30, 2024

MAJOR DISCOVERY! Found evidence of what I'm calling "The Great Shoelace Conspiracy." Department stores consistently stock laces 3.7 inches longer than necessary. Why? What are they hiding? Have submitted grant proposal to investigate.

November 5, 2024

Organized the first underground meeting of the Secret Society of Serious Shoelace Studies (SSSSS). Attendance was low, possibly due to my insistence that all members demonstrate proficiency in at least seven historical knotting techniques. Their loss.

November 10, 2024

Tom asked why I needed a high-speed camera in the shoe rack. Sometimes I wonder if he's really committed to the advancement of aglet science at all.

November 15, 2024

Conducted blind study comparing emotional responses to various lacing patterns. Results inconclusive after subjects became suspicious of being repeatedly asked to "share their feelings about these shoelaces." Must refine methodology.

November 20, 2024

Started work on my magnum opus: "Knot What You Think: A Complete History of Human Civilization Through Shoelace Analysis." Publishers seem skeptical. Clearly, they lack vision.

December 1, 2024

Emma's graduation approaching. Have prepared detailed analysis of optimal ribbon-tying techniques for diploma presentation. The school administration has preemptively banned me from "any unauthorized ribbon-related activities." Shortsighted.

Final Note: If anything happens to me, my collection of rare Victorian-era aglets should be donated to science. Not to that hack Professor String-Fuller – he wouldn't know a Dutch Square Knot from a Swiss Cross-Thread.

Addendum by Tom Knotting-Wells: Beatrice asked me to hide this journal in case "they" come looking for her revolutionary findings. I'm putting it in the sock drawer. That's the last place she'd look.

Chopstick Juggling

In the carefully manicured suburbs of central Texas—where ambition often manifests itself in curious ways—there resided one Simon Lynch, a gentleman whose relationship with practical reality might best be described as tentative. It was during one of those quintessentially American gatherings, where conversation flows as freely as suburban wisdom, that Simon's latest endeavor took root. His friend Dan, a man whose own grasp of human capability remained admirably grounded, had made what would prove to be a fateful observation about the universal accessibility of juggling.

The suggestion, innocuous as desert rain, settled into Simon's consciousness with the persistence of a summer dust storm. But where Dan had intended to direct his friend's attention toward the traditional implements of the juggler's art—spherical objects of predictable trajectory—Simon's mind wandered toward more exotic horizons. His focus settled, with what those who knew him would recognize as characteristic peculiarity, upon chopsticks.

The procurement phase of Simon's new obsession followed a pattern familiar to students of American suburban mythology. The local Asian market, an establishment whose proprietors had weathered countless cultural misunderstandings with stoic grace, found itself providing Simon with what might be termed an excessive quantity of wooden chopsticks—one hundred pairs, to be precise. The transaction raised eyebrows among the regular patrons, who recognized in Simon's enthusiasm the particular fervor of the newly converted.

Simon's preparation of his practice space revealed much about both his character and his previous experiences with domestic mishap. With the methodical attention of one who has learned from past catastrophe, he cleared the living room of breakables, positioning a mattress with the strategic consideration normally reserved for military defensive installations. The arrangement spoke eloquently of lessons learned through what his wife Twilla would later refer to as "the drone incident."

The internet, that vast repository of human knowledge and question-able wisdom, proved surprisingly reticent on the specific art of chopstick juggling. Simon found himself adrift in a digital sea of flaming torches and chainsaw tutorials, none of which quite addressed his particular needs. Like many pioneers before him, he was forced to adapt existing knowledge to new circumstances, though perhaps with less success than the original pathfinders of the American West.

His first attempt at mastery produced results that would have fascinated students of both physics and human psychology. The chopstick's trajec-tory, while impressive in its ambition, demonstrated a profound disregard for both Simon's intended path and basic principles of aerodynamics. Its collision with the ceiling fan resulted in minor architectural modifications that would later require professional attention.

Twilla, whose role in this domestic drama combined elements of wit-ness, historian, and prophet, observed these proceedings with the resigned wisdom of long experience. Her reference to the drone incident—an event that had achieved near-mythical status in local neighborhood chroni-cles—carried the weight of both historical record and gentle warning. The Smiths, whose garage roof had provided the final resting place for that particular adventure, still spoke of it during block parties with a mixture of amusement and lingering concern.

The family cat, Smurf—whose ancestors had surely witnessed similar human follies in more ancient settings—maintained a careful vigil from various strategic positions around the room. His eventual departure from the scene spoke volumes about both feline wisdom and self-preservation instincts.

The arrival of young Bethany into this tableau of determined practice and scattered wooden implements provided a moment of generational perspective. Her reaction—a mixture of teenage embarrassment and genuine concern—reflected the eternal dynamic between parent and child, particularly when the parent in question has decided to master an improbable skill involving dining implements.

The culmination of Simon's efforts arrived during a dinner party that included the formidable presence of Aunt Margaret, a woman whose standards of proper behavior had been set during a more restrained era. Simon's performance—two chopsticks describing perfect parabolic arcs before returning to his waiting hands—met with a silence that experienced anthropologists would have found worthy of detailed study.

Aunt Margaret's suggestion of knitting as an alternative pursuit carried with it generations of social commentary, delivered with the precise diplomatic skill of one who has navigated countless family gatherings. Her words, like many before them, would join the growing anthology of gentle attempts to redirect Simon's creative energies toward less hazardous pursuits.

Yet in the quiet aftermath of the evening, as Simon performed the ritual cleaning of dinner dishes, his spirit remained undiminished. In the tradition of countless American dreamers before him, he had pursued an improbable goal with more enthusiasm than skill, and in doing so, had added another chapter to the ongoing chronicle of suburban aspiration. The scattered chopsticks around his home stood as small wooden monuments to the enduring human desire to master the unnecessary, to pursue the improbable, and to occasionally worry the cat.

Whether the world was ready for chopstick juggling remained an open question, but Simon Lynch had already moved on to contemplating his next improbable achievement. Smurf, watching from his perch atop the refrigerator, seemed to suggest that some questions are better left unanswered.

The Lost Art of Paper Clip Sculpting

In the meticulous world of paper clip artistry, where masterpieces are measured in millimeters and careers can bend or break with a single twist, Dr. Claire "Steady Hands" Clipworth has spent three decades documenting what she calls "the renaissance of office supply sculpture." From her studio at the Institute of Miniature Metallurgy (IMM), she oversees what many consider the art form's golden age.

The taxonomy of paper clip sculpture reveals two distinct schools: the Architectural Innovators (Clippus structuralis), and the avant-garde Free Form Expressionists (Clippus abstractus). Each school maintains its own techniques, aesthetic philosophies, and deeply held beliefs about the true nature of paper clip manipulation.

Consider the case of Marcus "Wire Whisperer" Chen, whose paper clip recreation of the Eiffel Tower earned him international acclaim. "People think it's just about bending metal," he explains, delicately adjusting a microscopic flying buttress. "But at this level, you're really engineering on a molecular level."

The equipment requirements for elite paper clip sculpting have evolved dramatically. The Basic Artist's Kit, as mandated by IMM standards, includes micro-pliers, calibrated tension meters, and what artists call a "crisis kit" – specialized tools for unbending catastrophic mistakes. Advanced sculptors often add controversial equipment like the "Molecular Stress Analyzer" and humidity-controlled display cases.

Field research has revealed fascinating regional variations in technique. The German school emphasizes geometric precision, while Japanese masters focus on organic forms through their patented "Zen Bend" method. Meanwhile, the emerging Brazilian style combines elements of both, creating what experts call "industrial poetry in motion."

Dr. Heinrich von Clippenheim, author of "The Perfect Bend: Psychology of Miniature Metallurgy," has identified distinct personality types among artists. "The 'Technical Perfectionists' approach each clip like an engineer," he notes, "while the 'Intuitive Shapers' claim they can feel the metal's natural inclinations."

The economic implications of paper clip art cannot be ignored. The professional circuit, sponsored by leading office supply manufacturers, offers substantial prizes. "Last year's Grand Prix winner took home $20,000 and a lifetime supply of premium stainless steel clips," reveals Timothy Wire, CEO of Elite Office Artistry International.

Recent technological developments have sparked intense debate within the community. The introduction of computer-aided design tools has traditionalists concerned. "If you need more than your hands and your vision, you're in the wrong art form," argues Maria Bendez, holder of the current record for smallest recognizable sculpture.

For now, the elite world of paper clip sculpting continues to evolve, pushing the boundaries of human precision and creativity. As Marcus Chen likes to say while organizing his collection of rare vintage clips, "In life, as in paper clip art, true mastery lies not in the metal, but in the vision that bends it."

The Napkin Whisperer

In the concerned world of parental observation, where success is traditionally measured in career choices and grandchildren, Margaret and Robert Chen watch with growing bewilderment as their eldest son Marcus, once destined for medical school, disappears deeper into what he calls "the transcendent art of napkin manipulation."

"It started innocently enough," Margaret explains, serving tea in their perfectly normal dining room, where every napkin remains deliberately unfolded. "He was always neat, always particular about table settings. But then he started spending his medical school fund on imported linen and something called a humidity-controlled pressing chamber."

The Chen family has reluctantly learned to classify their son's obsession into what they call "phases of escalating concern": the Early Warning Signs (coming home with callused fingertips), the Intervention Stage (converting his bedroom into a "napkin meditation space"), and the Final Acceptance (when he legally changed his middle name to "The Napkin Whisperer").

Robert, a pragmatic accountant, maintains detailed records of their son's descent into napkin artistry. "Look at these expenses," he sighs, opening a spreadsheet labeled 'Marcus's Folly.' "Who pays $500 for a single napkin? Apparently, it's 'museum-grade Belgian linen' - whatever that means."

The turning point came during what the family now calls "The Christmas Incident." Marcus transformed their holiday dinner into what he termed a "performative napkin installation." Aunt Betty still refuses to attend family gatherings after her napkin "achieved spontaneous geometric transcendence" during the soup course.

Equipment began arriving daily: calibrated pressing tools, the mysterious "Fiber Stress Analyzer," and what Marcus insists on calling his "meditation station." His younger sister Jenny maintains a photo diary she titles "Things That Aren't Medical Instruments in My Brother's Room."

"We tried understanding," Margaret admits, showing a drawer full of crumpled self-help books about supporting your adult child's creative journey. "We attended his first exhibition at the International Napkin Arts

Symposium. Robert even attempted to fold a basic swan, though we don't talk about the resulting visit to the emergency room."

Family reunions have become an exercise in creative storytelling for the Chens. Each relative seems to require a different explanation for Marcus's chosen profession:

"So, Marcus," Aunt Betty begins, her voice tinged with concern, "how's the... napkin business going?"

Marcus's eyes light up. "Oh, Aunt Betty, it's transcendent! Just last week, I achieved a breakthrough in the triple-inverse pleat that's revolutionizing the industry!"

Betty nods vaguely while clutching her sensible paper napkin, shooting a desperate glance at Margaret.

Robert has developed a series of increasingly desperate professional descriptions: "He's in table aesthetics management." "He's a dining fabric consultant." "He works in hospitality presentation optimization." "He's an artisan of ephemeral textile sculptures." Finally, exasperated, he blurts out, "He's... he's... well, he folds napkins, Helen, what do you want me to say?"

The annual Chen family Thanksgiving has become particularly challenging. Uncle George, a retired steelworker, still introduces Marcus as "our doctor-to-be" despite the prominent napkin sculpture garden now occupying the family room. Marcus responds by creating increasingly elaborate centerpieces that his mother describes as "crying out for help in starched linen form."

"The worst part," Margaret confides during the cleanup of their latest family gathering, "is when they ask to see his work. You try explaining why someone would pay $5,000 for what Cousin Phil keeps calling 'that wrinkled thing in the corner.' It's not wrinkled, Phil - it's a quantum exploration of non-Euclidean fabric topology. Or so Marcus keeps telling us ."

The family has developed a code system for managing these situations. "Code White" means Marcus is about to launch into his lecture on the historical significance of the triple-inverse pleat. "Code Linen" indicates he's reaching for his portable humidifier and demonstration napkins. "Code Origami" is reserved for full emergencies, usually involving impromptu workshops with unwilling relatives.

Grandma Chen remains the only family member who's found a way to cope. "Oh, let the boy fold," she says, while discretely using her napkin to actually wipe her mouth, much to Marcus's visible distress. "Your grandfather used to collect vintage bottle caps. At least napkins are flat."

As Robert concludes at each gathering, usually after his third glass of coping mechanism, "Well, at least he's not living in our basement. He has his own humidity-controlled studio apartment now."

Margaret has even started a support group called "My Child, The Artist?" which meets monthly in the local library's craft room. "It helps to talk with other parents," she explains, carefully avoiding the origami instruction books in the reference section. "The Hendersons' daughter is a professional bubble wrap popper, so really, we got off easy."

As for Marcus, he remains blissfully unaware of his family's ongoing concerns, too absorbed in his latest project - a wedding commission featuring what he calls "quantum-entangled napkin pairs." His parents have decided not to ask what that means.

"Mom, Dad," Marcus exclaims, his eyes shining with excitement, "you won't believe what I've discovered! By folding these napkins in perfect synchronization, they maintain their connection even when separated. It's a metaphor for marriage, don't you see?"

Margaret and Robert exchange a look that speaks volumes. "That's... wonderful, dear," Margaret manages, while Robert mutters something about checking the wine cellar.

For now, the Chens have reached an uneasy truce with their son's chosen path. They've learned to warn dinner guests about spontaneous napkin demonstrations and keep a supply of paper napkins hidden in the garage. As Robert often says while reviewing Marcus's latest competition expenses, "At least he's not into competitive tow wrestling like the Wilsons' boy."

On a quiet Sunday afternoon, as Margaret watches Marcus meticulously press a stack of fine linen napkins, she reflects on their journey. "You know, Marcus," she says softly, "I may not always understand your passion, but I'm proud of the dedication you show to your art."

Marcus looks up, a rare moment of connection passing between them. "Thanks, Mom," he replies, a smile spreading across his face. "Want to learn a simple swan fold?"

Margaret hesitates, then nods. "Why not? But let's start with paper, shall we?"

In life, as in napkin folding, true mastery lies not in forcing the fabric, but in discovering the form it wishes to become

Competitive Pencil Sharpening

In the high-stakes world of competitive pencil sharpening, where victories are measured in microns and careers can be dulled by a single overzealous twist, the pursuit of the perfect point has evolved into a sophisticated art form. Dr. Marcus Graphite, director of the International Pencil Sharpening Institute (IPSI), has spent twenty-five years documenting what he terms "the atomic age of apex achievement."

The taxonomy of competitive sharpening reveals two distinct schools: the Traditional Rotarians (Grafitus manualis) and Electric Precision School (Grafitus electricus). Each group maintains its own techniques, training regimens, and deeply held beliefs about the true nature of pencil perfection.

Consider the case of Janet "Steady-Hand" Williams, fifteen-time world champion in the Manual Division. "People think it's just about turning the pencil," she explains, demonstrating her signature triple-rotation technique on a pristine Ticonderoga No. 2. "But at this level, you're really conducting a symphony of graphite and wood."

The equipment requirements for elite sharpening have evolved dramatically. The Basic Competition Kit, as mandated by IPSI regulations, includes a calibrated angle gauge, digital point measurement tools, and what practitioners call a "bleeding kit" – bandages for the occasional overeager sharpener. Advanced competitors often add specialized equipment like the controversial "Graphite Whisper Listener" and humidity-controlled storage cases.

Field research has revealed fascinating regional variations in technique. The Japanese school emphasizes minimal wood removal, while German competitors focus on structural integrity through their patented "Drei-Punkt" method. Meanwhile, the emerging Brazilian style combines elements of both, creating what experts call a "samba of symmetry."

The social hierarchy within competitive sharpening is rigidly structured. Novices begin in the "Blunt Division," working with carpenter pencils before advancing to standard No. 2s. Only after years of training can they attempt the prestigious "Technical Perfect Point" category, where points are measured to within 0.001 millimeters.

Dr. Helena von Sharpenstein, author of "Point of No Return: The Psychology of Competitive Sharpening," has identified distinct personality types among competitors. "The 'Precision Perfectionists' approach each pencil like a surgeon," she notes, "while the 'Intuitive Artisans' claim they can feel the perfect point emerging through the wood grain."

Economic implications of competitive sharpening have not gone unnoticed. The professional circuit, sponsored by leading pencil manufacturers, offers substantial prizes. "Last year's Grand Prix winner took home $50,000 and a lifetime supply of premium cedar-cased pencils," reveals Timothy Lead, CEO of Premium Points International.

Environmental factors play a crucial role in competition outcomes. The World Championships maintain strict controls for temperature, humidity, and even barometric pressure. "A single degree of temperature difference can affect wood density," explains Dr. Graphite. "We've seen careers ended by unexpected climate variations."

Recent technological developments have sparked intense debate within the community. The introduction of titanium-bladed manual sharpeners has traditionalists crying foul. "If you need more than steel and skill, you're in the wrong sport," argues Vladimir Petroshenko, holder of the current speed-sharpening record.

Training regimens for competitive sharpeners border on monastic dedication. The legendary "500 Hundred Points of Light Hardness" exercise requires aspirants to sharpen 50 pencils daily for 10 days, achieving identical points on each. "It's not about the pencils," explains Master Trainer Wei Chang. "It's about finding the perfect point within yourself."

The psychological toll of competition can be severe. Sports psychologist Dr. Sarah Leadbetter has documented what she calls " among retired champions. "The sound of a pencil sharpener can trigger intense emotional responses," she notes. "These athletes live on the cutting edge, literally and figuratively."

As interest in competitive sharpening grows, concerns about doping have emerged. The World Anti-Doping Agency for Pencil Sports (WADAPS) now tests for substances that might steady hands or enhance visual acuity. "The integrity of the point must be matched by the integrity of the sport," insists WADAPS director James Holbrook.

For now, the elite world of competitive pencil sharpening continues to evolve, pushing the boundaries of human precision and patience. As Janet Williams likes to say while polishing her collection of vintage sharpeners, "In life, as in sharpening, true perfection lies not in the point itself, but in the endless pursuit of it."

The Great Pillow Schism: A Tale of Two Leagues

In the high-stakes world of competitive pillow fighting, where victories are measured in feathers and careers can be flattened by a single miscalculated swing, Dweebie "The Cushion Crusher" Towns has spent five years documenting what she calls "the ultimate test of soft-weapon mastery." From her position at the International Pillow Fighting Federation (IPFF), she oversees what many consider the sport's burgeoning golden age.

The taxonomy of competitive pillow fighting reveals four distinct schools: the Speed Swingers (Pillowus velocitus), the Power Puffers (Pillowus maximus), the Tactical Technicians (Pillowus strategicus), and the enigmatic Stealth Strikers (Pillowus silentius). Each group maintains its own techniques, training regimens, and deeply held beliefs about the true path to pillow supremacy. The Stealth Strikers are particularly known for their "Ghost Strike" technique, where competitors claim they never see the pillow coming until it's too late.

Consider the case of Marcus "The Mattress Menace" Chen, whose revolutionary "Tornado Technique" changed the sport forever. "People think it's just about swinging pillows," he explains, demonstrating his signature triple-rotation strike on a practice dummy. "But at this level, you're really conducting a symphony of aerodynamics and down-force physics."

The equipment requirements for elite pillow fighting have evolved dramatically. The Basic Competition Kit includes calibrated pillow pressure gauges, feather dispersal monitors, and what practitioners call a "recovery station" – specialized equipment for post-match pillow rehabilitation. Advanced fighters often add controversial equipment like the "Down Force Calculator 21.5" and climate-controlled pillow storage units.

Dr. Heinrich von Pillowstein, author of "The Perfect Strike: Psychology of Pillow Combat," has identified distinct fighting styles among competitors. "The 'Aggressive Stuffers' focus on brute force," he notes, "while the 'Strategic Flappers' believe true mastery lies in calculated feather distribution."

Training regimens for competitive pillow fighters border on the extreme. The legendary "Twenty Swings" exercise requires aspirants to perfect their technique through progressive resistance training. "By swing 5," explains Master Trainer Yuki Pillowaki, "most students can detect pillow filling density by sound alone."

Environmental factors play a crucial role in competition outcomes. The World Championships maintain strict controls for air movement, humidity, and feather loft. "A single draft can alter pillow trajectory," explains Dr. Downsworth. "We've seen championships decided by unexpected air conditioning gusts."

The schism in professional pillow fighting began in 2019 when the breakaway Progressive Pillow Fighting League (PPFL) challenged the IPFF's traditional standards. "It's about evolution," explains Regina "Iron Pillow" Nowser, PPFL Commissioner. "The sport can't grow if we remain stuck in the past, clinging to outdated pillow-to-handle ratios."

At the heart of the controversy lies what enthusiasts call "The Great Stuffing Debate." The IPFF maintains strict regulations: competition pillows must measure exactly 20x26 inches with a 4-inch handle, filled exclusively with Hungarian goose down. The PPFL, in contrast, permits synthetic fills and advocates for their controversial "freestyle sizing" approach, allowing handles up to 6 inches and pillow dimensions that can reach a shocking 24x30 inches.

"It's not pillow fighting anymore," scoffs Traditional League Chairman Herbert "The Traditionalist" Thompson, clutching a regulation-size pillow. "What's next? Memory foam? Decorative tassels? Some lines cannot be crossed."

The rivalry has split the pillow fighting community. Veteran fighters like Marcus Chen remain loyal to IPFF standards, while younger competitors are drawn to the PPFL's more dynamic style. "The longer handle allows for techniques that were impossible under traditional rules," argues Chen's former student, Sarah "The Innovator" Wong, who defected to the PPFL in 2021.

International competitions have become particularly contentious, with both leagues claiming to represent the sport's true spirit. The 2023 Global Pillow Fighting Championships featured parallel tournaments, each crowning their own champion and leading to what journalists called "The Double Down Debacle."

Dr. Downsworth, attempting to mediate between the factions, has proposed a unified set of standards she calls "The Goldilocks Protocol" – not too big, not too small, but just right. Her suggestion of a 5-inch handle compromise was met with simultaneous outrage from both camps.

For now, the sport remains divided, with both leagues claiming record attendance and growing fan bases. The IPFF continues to host its "Classic Series" tournaments in traditional venues like hotel ballrooms and conference centers, while the PPFL stages more theatrical events in converted warehouses with elaborate lighting and synthetic feather effects.

"Perhaps there's room for both approaches," muses Dr. Downsworth, examining a collection of championship pillows from both leagues. "After all, in the end, we're all just trying to perfect the art of hitting each other with bedroom accessories."

Recent developments suggest a possible reconciliation. The newly formed Joint Pillow Advisory Committee (JPAC) has proposed a series of exhibition matches featuring "hybrid rules" - though negotiations stalled over whether to use goose down or hypoallergenic fill for the historic first meet.

As Marcus Chen likes to say while training the next generation of fighters, "In life, as in pillow fighting, true mastery lies not in the size of your pillow, but in the power of your swing." Meanwhile, underground "outlaw" pillow fighting continues to grow, with controversial use of decorative pillows and forbidden techniques like the "Memory Foam Mayhem."

The future of professional pillow fighting remains as fluffy as its implements. Whether the sport will reunite under a single set of standards or continue along parallel paths is anyone's guess. But one thing remains certain: as long as there are pillows, there will be those who seek to master the art of wielding them in combat.

[Note: Three officials were lightly thumped during the writing

Extreme Competitive Eyebrow Dancing

Simon fresh off his "Chopstick Juggling" now is attempting the mastery over his supraorbital musculature would will lead him into one of the more curious competitive arenas of contemporary culture. Like the ancient pueblos of the Southwest, where each architectural feature served both practical and ceremonial purposes, Simon's eyebrows had long functioned as tools of domestic communication, particularly effective in expressing silent judgment over his daughter Bethany's sartorial choices and his wife Trilla's peculiar devotion to irregularly formed tubers.

The catalyst for Simon's transformation from casual facial expressionist to competitive athlete arrived in the form of a modest announcement at the local community center—an establishment that, like the trading posts of old, served as a nexus for cultural exchange and social innovation. The flyer, promising instruction in "Extreme Competitive Eyebrow Dancing," spoke to something deep within Simon's soul, much as the desert winds speak to those who know how to listen.

The training ground for this peculiar art form was the community center's multipurpose room, a space that, like the kivas of the ancient Pueblo peoples, served multiple ceremonial functions. Here gathered an assemblage of facial athletes whose diversity would have delighted any social anthropologist: a youth whose spiked hair suggested rebellion against conventional grooming standards; an elderly woman whose countenance carried the gravitas of one who had perfected the art of facial disapproval over decades; and Greg, Simon's neighbor, whose eyebrow movements had somehow developed a curious synchronicity with the rhythms of classic rock—a phenomenon worthy of detailed academic study.

Presiding over this gathering was Marcel Dupont, known in professional circles as "The Brow Maestro," a title that carried the weight of ancient tribal wisdom combined with modern competitive achievement. His introduction to the assembled aspirants came in the form of a single, precisely executed eyebrow arch—a gesture that, like the petroglyphs of the Southwest, conveyed volumes of meaning to those versed in its interpretation.

The training regimen that followed would have fascinated students of both physical culture and social anthropology. The double brow flutter—a movement requiring precise control over the corrugator supercilii muscles—emerged as the foundational technique of the discipline. Simon's initial attempts at this maneuver bore more resemblance to arachnid-avoidance behavior than to the controlled artistry required by the competitive circuit.

Trilla, whose role in this narrative combined elements of witness, historian, and skeptic, observed her husband's transformation with the measured patience of one who had weathered previous enthusiasms like Chopstick Juggling. Her collection of morphologically distinct potatoes served as silent witnesses to the household's tolerance for unconventional pursuits.

The regional championships, held in the civic center—a modern equivalent of ancient ceremonial grounds—drew practitioners of the art from across the territory. Competitors such as Felicity "Fierce Brows" McGuire and Carlos "El Capitan Ceja" demonstrated their mastery with the sort of precision that anthropologists might compare to the rain dances of southwestern tribes, where every movement carried significance.

Simon's performance that evening, while not achieving championship status, earned him recognition for "Most Enthusiastic Eyebrow Performance"—a distinction that spoke to the American tradition of celebrating effort as much as achievement. The golden eyebrow trophy, positioned carefully among Trilla's tubercular collection, stood as a testament to this curious intersection of suburban ambition and physical artistry.

The mirror in the Lynch household now served a dual purpose: both as a practical tool for daily grooming and as a training ground for future competitive endeavors. Simon's practiced movements before it, particularly his signature slow lift, represented the continuation of a tradition that, while perhaps not as ancient as the pottery-making techniques of the Pueblo peoples, nevertheless spoke to humanity's endless capacity for creating new forms of artistic expression.

In the end, like many American suburban pioneers before him, Simon Lynch had carved out his own niche in the cultural landscape. His journey from casual eyebrow manipulator to competitive facial athlete illustrated a fundamental truth about contemporary suburban life: that greatness often lies not in the achievement itself, but in the willingness to pursue excellence in even the most unlikely of arenas.

The trophy on the mantel, catching the light alongside Trilla's peculiar potato collection, stood as a modern artifact—evidence for future anthropologists studying the remarkable ways in which late-twentieth-century suburban dwellers chose to distinguish themselves in the endless quest for meaning and achievement.

Mastering the Art of Competitive Staring

In the intense world of competitive staring, where victories are measured in microseconds and careers can be blinked away in an instant, Dr. Iris "Steady Eyes" Visionsworth has spent twenty years documenting what she terms "the ultimate test of ocular fortitude." From her position at the International Staring Society (ISS), she oversees what many consider the sport's golden age.

The taxonomy of competitive staring reveals three distinct schools: the Zen Masters (Oculus tranquilus), the Intimidators (Oculus dominatus), and the controversial Psychological Warfare specialists (Oculus manipulatus). Each group maintains its own techniques, training regimens, and deeply held beliefs about the true path to unblinking victory.

Consider the case of James "Stone Face" Peterson, current world record holder with an unbroken stare of 47 minutes and 23 seconds. "Most people think it's just about keeping your eyes open," he explains, demonstrating his signature "Void Gaze" technique. "But at this level, you're really engaging in psychological warfare through pupillary dominance."

The equipment requirements for elite staring have evolved dramatically. The Basic Competition Kit, as mandated by ISS regulations, includes calibrated eye moisture meters, light intensity controls, and what practitioners call an "emergency kit" – specialized eye drops for post-match recovery. Advanced competitors often add controversial equipment like the "Humidity Shield 2B" and temperature-controlled goggles for training.

Dr. Helena von Eyenstein, author of "The Unblinking Truth: Psychology of Competitive Staring," has identified distinct personality types among competitors. "The 'Zen Staters' achieve victory through mental transcendence," she notes, "while the 'Aggressive Gazers' rely on psychological intimidation."

The social impact of competitive staring extends beyond the sport itself. Corporate training programs now include "Power Staring" workshops, and the annual Global Stare-Down Championship draws thousands. "Last year's finals lasted nearly two hours," reports Timothy Blink, CEO of Elite Vision Sports International.

Recent technological developments have sparked intense debate. The introduction of automated blink detection systems has traditionalists concerned. "If you need more than two human judges and a stopwatch, you're missing the soul of the sport," argues Maria "Eagle Eyes" Rodriguez, holder of the current women's world record.

Training regimens for competitive starers border on monastic dedication. The legendary "Hundred Yard Stare" exercise requires practitioners to focus on distant objects for increasing durations. "By week six," explains Master Trainer Wei "No Blink" Chang, "most students can read a newspaper through their tears."

Environmental factors play a crucial role in competition outcomes. The World Championships maintain strict controls for air movement and humidity levels. "A single draft can end a career-defining stare," explains Dr. Visionsworth. "We've seen champions fall to an ill-timed air conditioning burst."

For now, the elite world of competitive staring continues to evolve, pushing the boundaries of human endurance and psychological warfare. As James Peterson likes to say while practicing his thousand-yard stare, "In life, as in staring, victory lies not in the strength of your eyes, but in the power of your will to never blink first."

The Exit 47 Method: Bubble Wrap Popping

A REVOLITIONARY APPROACH TO COMPETITIVE BUBBLE WRAP

In the fluorescent-lit world of highway toll collection, where success is measured in correct change and careers can crumble with a single miscount, Eugene "Quick Hands" Kowalski has spent fifteen years developing what he calls "the ultimate fusion of occupational necessity and competitive bubble wrap popping." From his booth on Exit 47 of the New Jersey Turnpike, he revolutionized the sport with his groundbreaking "Toll Booth Technique."

"It all started with those padded envelopes," explains Kowalski, demonstrating his signature move during a quiet 3 AM shift. "When you're making change 40,000 times a day, you need something to keep your fingers nimble." His technique, which combines rapid-fire popping with precise coin-counting movements, has caught the attention of the International Bubble Wrap Institute (IBWI).

Dr. Victoria Bubbleworth, initially skeptical of Kowalski's unorthodox methods, now considers the Toll Booth Technique a legitimate fourth school of competitive popping. "He's merged the speed of the Velocity School with the precision of coin handling," she notes, studying recordings of Kowalski's technique. "The way he incorporates exact change into his popping patterns is nothing short of revolutionary."

The Toll Booth Technique requires specialized equipment beyond standard popping gear. Kowalski's Basic Kit includes a modified coin dispenser, calibrated bubble wrap strips cut to exact toll-lane width, and what he calls his "change integration station" – a custom-built practice area that simulates peak traffic conditions.

"Most poppers train in climate-controlled facilities," Kowalski explains, adjusting his booth's ancient heating unit. "But try maintaining perfect bubble tension when you're dealing with Jersey weather, exact change requirements, and someone honking because their E-ZPass isn't working. That's where real mastery develops."

His most controversial innovation involves what he terms "synchronized transaction popping" – a technique where each bubble pop corresponds to a specific denomination of change. "Quarters get a firm three-finger pop, nickels a quick thumb strike, and don't even get me started on handling seasonal toll adjustments," he says, demonstrating a particularly complex sequence involving five dollars in mixed change.

The Lincoln Tunnel controversy remains a sore point in competitive popping circles. Tommy "Three Lanes" DiMaggio claims he pioneered synchronized popping techniques during the tunnel's notorious 1989 traffic jams. "Kowalski's technique? Please," DiMaggio scoffs from his center booth. "We were doing double-pop toll returns before he could make change for a dollar."

The rivalry has spawned two distinct schools: the Exit 47 Expressionists (followers of Kowalski's fluid style) and the Tunnel Transit Technicians (DiMaggio's disciples). Each group maintains its own training methods, adapted to their unique traffic patterns.

"You can't compare tunnel popping to open-road technique," insists DiMaggio, demonstrating his signature "Tunnel Echo Enhancement" method. "We've got acoustics in here that Kowalski can only dream about. Every pop resonates with the souls of frustrated commuters."

Kowalski dismisses such claims. "The tunnel people think they're special because they work underground," he explains while executing a perfect five-dollar transaction sequence. "But try maintaining bubble integrity in direct sunlight during rush hour. That's where true mastery reveals itself."

The debate reached its peak during the 2023 Tri-State Transportation Authority Popping Championships. Kowalski's "Rush Hour Rhapsody" routine, featuring synchronized popping timed to actual traffic patterns, seemed unbeatable. Then DiMaggio unveiled his controversial "Tunnel Tension Symphony," incorporating echo effects and ventilation fan rhythms.

The judges' decision remains disputed. "They didn't account for ambient moisture conditions," Kowalski argues, pointing to his meticulously

maintained humidity logs. "Underground popping is basically environmental doping."

Meanwhile, a third faction has emerged from the George Washington
Bridge, claiming their elevation-based techniques represent the true future
of toll booth popping. "These guys arguing about tunnels and turnpikes,"
notes bridge operator Maria "High Rise" Rodriguez, "they're missing the
vertical dimension entirely."

For now, Kowalski continues refining his technique during the quiet
overnight shifts, each pop bringing him closer to what he calls "the perfect
fusion of transaction and tension release." As he likes to say while making
change for yet another twenty, "In life, as in bubble wrap, true satisfaction
comes not from the pop itself, but from the exact change you make along
the way."

[Note: Several sheets of bubble wrap were respectfully popped during
the writing of this article, all in strict accordance with Turnpike Authority
regulations.]

Extreme Thumb Wrestling

In the high-stakes world of competitive thumb wrestling, where victories are determined by milliseconds and careers can pivot on a single opposable digit, Dr. Thomas "Lightning Thumb" McGregor has spent two decades documenting what he calls "the ultimate test of manual dexterity." From his position at the Global Thumb Wrestling Federation (GTWF), he oversees what many consider the sport's platinum age.

The taxonomy of thumb wrestling reveals three distinct schools: the Speed Strikers (Pollicus velocitus), the Power Grapplers (Pollicus maximus), and the enigmatic Technical Tacticians (Pollicus strategicus). Each group maintains its own training methods, combat philosophies, and deeply held beliefs about the true path to thumb supremacy.

Consider the case of Sarah "The Hammer" Rodriguez, current world champion and holder of the fastest pin record at 0.73 seconds. "People think it's just about thumb strength," she explains, demonstrating her signature "Cobra Strike" technique. "But at this level, you're really playing four-dimensional chess with your digit."

The equipment requirements for elite thumb wrestling have evolved dramatically. The Basic Competition Kit, as mandated by GTWF regulations, includes regulation thumb guards, grip enhancers, and what competitors call a "recovery station" – specialized equipment for post-match thumb rehabilitation. Advanced wrestlers often add controversial equipment like the "Reflex Maximizer 3000" and climate-controlled thumb warmers.

Dr. Heinrich von Thumbenstein, author of "The Perfect Pin: Psychology of Digit Combat," has identified distinct fighting styles among competitors. "The 'Aggressive Pinners' rely on explosive power," he notes, "while the 'Strategic Circlers' prefer to wear down their opponents through superior positioning."

The economic implications of competitive thumb wrestling have become significant. The professional circuit, sponsored by leading sports equipment manufacturers, offers substantial prizes. "Last year's World Championship winner took home $35,000 and a custom-designed gold thumb guard," reveals Timothy Digits, CEO of Elite Thumb Sports International.

Training regimens for competitive thumb wrestlers border on the extreme. The legendary "Thousand Pins" exercise requires aspirants to perform one hundred pins daily for ten days straight. "By day seven," explains Master Trainer Yuki Thumbaki, "most students can't operate a smartphone."

For now, the elite world of thumb wrestling continues to evolve, pushing the boundaries of human reflexes and determination. As Sarah Rodriguez likes to say while icing her championship thumb, "In life, as in thumb wrestling, true victory lies not in the strength of your digit, but in the power of your spirit."

When Puzzle Pieces Vanish

In the dusty world of puzzle piece production, where quality was once measured by the precision of die-cuts and careers spanned generations of cardboard crafting, Herbert "Old Puzzler" Jameson has spent fifty years documenting what he calls "the great escape." From his converted garden shed in Sheffield, surrounded by thousands of production samples saved from the quality control bin at the Fitwell Puzzle Factory (1954-1998), he studies the curious case of pieces that choose to vanish.

The taxonomy of missing puzzle pieces, carefully noted in Herb's grease-stained production logs, reveals five distinct categories: the Factory Fleers (Puzzlus escapus), the Box Bolters (Puzzlus fugitivus), the Assembly Avoiders (Puzzlus reluctantus), the Quality Control Questioners (Puzzlus rebellius), and most mysteriously, the Production Line Phantoms (Puzzlus phantasmus) - pieces that vanish before they're even cut.

"I first noticed it during the night shift in '73," Herb explains, thumbing through decades of meticulously maintained shift reports. "Pieces would simply vanish between the cutting press and the sorting bin. Perfect pieces, mind you - I checked every die myself." He gestures to his collection of vintage cutting dies, each labeled with dates and mysterious notations about "escape probability factors."

Over the years, Herb's observation equipment evolved from simple tally counters and carbon paper to sophisticated tools like the Conveyor Belt Monitor and the Die-Cut Deviation Detector. His pride and joy was the "early warning system" - a network of bells attached to sorting bins that chimed when pieces attempted escape.

Dr. von Puzzlenstein once dismissed Herb's theories as "the ramblings of an overworked line manager," until Herb revealed forty years of production data showing consistent patterns of disappearance. "It always starts with the edge pieces," Herb insists, pointing to charts showing higher escape rates during full moons. "They're the clever ones - they organize the getaways for the others."

"Tea break patterns are crucial to understanding piece behavior," Herb explains, pulling out a tea-stained notebook labeled 'Break Time Observations 1975-1998'. "The pieces seemed to know exactly when the quality control inspector went for his cuppa. That's when most escapes occurred - between 10:17 and 10:32 AM, precise as clockwork."

Herb's most controversial findings involve what he calls "The Great Tea Break Theory." Every day for twenty-three years, Herb documented piece disappearances relative to the strength of the factory's tea brewing. "Strong Yorkshire Tea days saw 47% fewer escape attempts," he notes, tapping a graph drawn on the back of an old production schedule. "But when young Thompson started bringing that fancy herbal stuff in '82, well, chaos ensued. Lost three entire landscape collections that month alone."

The factory's break room became his primary observation post. He installed a complex system of mirrors to monitor the production line while appearing to do his crossword.

"The pieces get crafty when they think no one's watching," he whispers, revealing a hidden compartment in his thermos where he kept his observation equipment. "Had to be subtle about it - management already thought I was odd for naming the cutting dies." Herb's research suggests distinct patterns in piece behavior:

- Morning shifts showed higher escape rates, particularly during the first tea break

- Pieces from scenic puzzles attempted escape more often than abstract designs

- Sky pieces were particularly flighty, while grass sections showed more loyalty

- Pieces would often coordinate their disappearances with the factory whistle

"It's not just about the timing," he insists, showing visitor's logs he kept disguised as production reports. "You had to understand their motivation. Every piece that vanished had a story. Some were just adventurous, others were protesting poor quality control standards, and a few - well, a few just couldn't bear the thought of being part of a Thomas Kinkade."

His most treasured evidence comes from the winter of '89, when he noticed pieces studying the factory floor plan posted by the fire exit. "Next day, half a shipment of 'Cozy Cottage' puzzles vanished. Left nothing but a few cottage windows and what I swear was a tiny thank-you note."

The factory closed in '98, but Herb continues his research from home. His garden shed, which he calls the "Institute of Retired Puzzle Piece Behavior," houses decades of documentation. "Sometimes at night," he confides, "I still hear them plotting. Just last week, a piece from a 1962 'English Countryside' set finally made its bid for freedom. Had to admire its patience."

Now retired, Herb spends his days cataloging what he calls "the ones that got away," maintaining detailed files on every piece that ever vanished under his watch. His garden shed has become a pilgrimage site for other re-tired puzzle factory workers who've harbored similar suspicions but never dared to speak up.

"The young folks at these fancy puzzle research institutes, with their quantum theories and metaphysical hypotheses," he muses, sipping tea from his trusted observation thermos, "they're missing the obvious. It's not about transcendence or philosophical void - it's about tea breaks and freedom."

His final production log entry, dated the day the factory closed, reads simply: "To all the pieces that chose their own path - I understand. I too am finally breaking free from my prescribed pattern." He keeps this log on his bedside table, next to a single puzzle piece from his very first shift in 1954 - the only piece, he claims, that ever tried to warn him about the others' escape plans.

"Some nights," Herb confides, locking up his shed filled with five decades of evidence, "I hear them having parties in there. And you know what? I don't begrudge them that. After thirty years of quality control, perhaps we all deserve to be a bit uncontrolled."

His last official statement on the matter, scribbled on the back of an old tea bag wrapper: "In puzzles, as in life, sometimes the pieces that go missing are simply the ones brave enough to write their own story."

Competitive Yodeling for Beginners

In the dimly lit basements of suburban Pittsburgh, an ancient Alpine art form is experiencing an unlikely renaissance. Urban yodeling, known academically as Subterranean Vocal Oscillation (SVO), has emerged as a curious blend of traditional Swiss techniques and modern acoustic adaptation. Dr. Helga Warblestein, author of "Basement Echoes: The Underground Yodeling Movement," has documented this phenomenon for the past decade.

"What fascinates me," says Dr. Warblestein, adjusting her noise-canceling headphones, "is how the basement environment has created entirely new yodeling subspecies." She refers to the three distinct styles that have evolved: the Furnace Room Resonator (Yodelius basementus), the Laundry Day Harmonizer (Yodelius washeria), and the rare Storage Space Reverberator (Yodelius clutterus maximus).

Consider the case of Chuck Peterson, a former accountant from Altoona, who discovered his passion for basement yodeling after a particularly frustrating tax season. "The first time I let out a good 'yo-del-ay-hee-hoo' next to the water heater, the acoustics were life-changing," he recalls, demonstrating the technique that has since earned him the nickname "The Garden State Goatherd."

The fundamentals of basement yodeling require careful attention to environmental factors. Janet Murphy, leading instructor at the Suburban Alpine Arts Center (located in her split-level ranch home's basement), emphasizes the importance of proper positioning. "Stand three feet from the concrete wall, slightly angled toward the dehumidifier," she advises. "And never, ever yodel directly into the circuit breaker panel."

Equipment requirements for aspiring basement yodelers remain surprisingly minimal. Standard gear includes moisture-wicking lederhosen (to combat basement humidity), a headlamp (for power outage performances), and what practitioners call a "panic button" – a pre-recorded excuse to explain the sounds to concerned neighbors. Advanced yodelers often add specialized equipment like the "Echo-Enhancement Dryer Vent" and the controversial "Furnace Harmonizer 3000."

The social impact of this movement has been remarkable. The National Association of Basement Yodelers (NABY) reports a 300% increase in membership since 2020, though skeptics note this might correlate with increased time spent at home. Local chapters have sprung up across the country, with members gathering for what they call "Underground Echo Sessions."

Dr. Heinrich von Trappist, leading researcher in Domestic Alpine Studies, has identified unique regional variations. "East Coast basement yodelers tend toward what we call 'radiator rhythm,'" he explains, "while West Coast practitioners have developed a distinct 'earthquake-ready vibrato.'" His research team has documented over 47 basement-specific yodeling techniques, including the "Washing Machine Waltz" and the "Pilot Light Pitch."

The technical challenges of basement yodeling have led to innovative solutions. Martha Svenson, a retired acoustical engineer, developed the "Basement Yodel Dampening System" after receiving multiple noise complaints. "It's basically egg cartons and old moving blankets arranged in a specific pattern," she reveals. "But don't let its simplicity fool you – it's all about the angular placement."

Community response to basement yodeling has been mixed. The Neighborhood Association of Greater Altoona issued guidelines suggesting "yodeling hours" between 10 AM and 4 PM, while some municipalities have begun requiring "basement yodeling permits" for practice sessions exceeding 30 minutes.

For serious practitioners, progression through the ranks follows a strict hierarchy. Beginners start with the "Whisper Yodel" (practicing near storage boxes for sound absorption), advancing to intermediate levels like the "Dryer Cycle Duet" and finally achieving mastery with the coveted "Full Basement Resonance."

Health professionals have noted unexpected benefits. Dr. Sarah Lung-worth's study "Respiratory Benefits of Subterranean Yodeling" suggests that the combination of basement humidity and vocal exercise may improve lung capacity, though she cautions against excessive exposure to dryer lint.

As this uniquely American adaptation of Alpine culture continues to evolve, one thing remains clear: in basements across the country, the hills are alive with the sound of music – albeit slightly damper and more echoey than their Swiss counterparts.

As Chuck Peterson likes to say, while adjusting his battery-powered headlamp, "You haven't really yodeled until you've yodeled next to a hot water heater." Words that resonate, quite literally, through the hearts and basements of urban yodeling enthusiasts everywhere.

Lost Socks: Where Do They Go

In the cozy world of domestic research, where success is measured in matched pairs and careers can span generations of laundry days, Daphne "The Sock Whisperer" Taylor has spent seventy-three years documenting what she calls "the great sock conspiracy." From her Victorian laundry room in Chelsea, where she maintains precisely eighteen clothes pegs per line (never seventeen or nineteen, as that upsets the socks), she conducts the world's longest-running study of sock behavior patterns.

"It all started in 1943," she explains, adjusting her flowered housecoat and offering tea in cups she swears affect sock behavior. "My husband's best Sunday sock vanished, only to reappear three months later wrapped around a cucumber in the garden. That's when I knew they were clever little blighters."

The taxonomy of sock disappearance, meticulously recorded in tea-stained notebooks, reveals what she calls "the sock personality spectrum." The Quick Vanishers (Sockus mysteriosus) disappear between the washer and the line, often while she's distracted by Mrs. Higgins' cat watching from next door. The Wandering Stragglers (Sockus vagabundus) turn up in odd places - inside Wellington boots, nestled in teapots, or inexplicably tangled in her knitting. Most mysterious are the Return Visitors (Sockus reappearus), which reappear years later, often during significant family events, as if they've been waiting for the perfect moment to make a dramatic entrance.

Daphne's research methods are as eccentric as they are thorough. Every Wednesday at precisely 3:47 PM (never 3:46 or 3:48, as socks are notoriously punctual), she conducts what she calls her "sock séance." The ritual involves arranging single socks in a perfect circle around her grandmother's Victorian tea service, playing a Rolling Stones record, and attempting to communicate with their missing mates.

"The music is crucial," she whispers, carefully positioning her favorite floral teacup exactly three inches from a lone argyle sock. "They're particularly partial to You Can't Always Wash What You Want,' though I've had some success with "Paint It Sock" during full moons."

Her most controversial technique involves what she calls "sock psychology." Each laundry day, she sets elaborate traps using her late husband's pipe tobacco as bait - a technique she swears once lured back an entire week's worth of missing socks during the winter of '62. "That was the Great Sock Return of 1962," she recalls, misty-eyed. "Though oddly, they all came back slightly different colors. Crafty things."

The garden plays a crucial role in her research. She's convinced that garden gnomes serve as sock guardians, and regularly rotates their positions to create what she calls "sock-safe corridors." Her prized gnome, Winston (named for his remarkable resemblance to Churchill), presides over a special sock recovery zone beneath the hydrangeas.

Her observations have led to several groundbreaking theories in the field of missing sock behavior. The "Tea Cozy Effect," as she terms it, suggests that socks are more likely to return when they smell brewing Earl Grey. Her "Biscuit Correlation Theory" proposes that digestives are more effective than rich tea biscuits at attracting wayward hosiery, though custard creams show promise in preliminary studies.

"It's all about creating the right atmosphere," she explains, arranging her collection of single socks by what she calls their "emotional temperature." "Socks are sensitive creatures. They can sense anxiety. That's why I always wear my lucky pearls when hanging out the washing. Helps them feel more at home, you see."

Her most recent discovery involves what she calls "sock telepathy." Every night at midnight, she reads bedtime stories to particularly recalcitrant single socks, claiming this practice has increased her recovery rate by thirty-seven percent. "They're especially fond of Agatha Christie," she confides. "Something about the mysteries speaks to their souls."

After seven decades of research, Mrs. Taylor's conclusions remain both profound and peculiar. "Every sock," she declares, pouring another cup of precisely steeped tea, "has its own destiny. Some are meant to stay, some to wander, and some..." she pauses dramatically, adjusting her pearls, "some are simply living more exciting lives than their owners."

Her legacy includes forty-three volumes of hand-written observations, a garden full of strategically placed gnomes, and what she claims is the world's largest collection of single socks (all meticulously labeled with their last known whereabouts). The local museum has expressed interest in her archives, though they remain puzzled by her insistence that the exhibits must be rotated according to the lunar calendar.

"In the end," she muses, gently stroking her cat Fluffy (whom she's convinced is the reincarnation of a particularly notorious sock thief from 1957), "perhaps we're asking the wrong question. It's not where the socks go, but why they choose to go there."

For now, the mystery continues, documented in tea-stained pages and whispered about at Women's Institute meetings. As Daphne often says while arranging her evening sock séance, "In life, as in laundry, some mysteries are better left unsolved – especially if you've got a good cup of tea and a biscuit to hand."

Mastering the Art of Competitive Yawning

In the high-stakes world of competitive yawning, where open mouths meet open minds, only the truly dedicated can hope to achieve greatness. As a sports journalist who has covered everything from professional napping to extreme couch-sitting, I can tell you that competitive yawning is where dreams are made – and promptly dozed through.

The sport traces its origins to a particularly boring afternoon in 1983, when a group of university students discovered they could weaponize their post-lecture fatigue. Since then, it has evolved into a sophisticated competitive discipline, complete with its own governing body: The International Federation of Yawning Athletes (IFYA).

Dr. Sandra "Sleepy" Martinez, a leading expert in competitive yawning and author of "Why Am I Even Writing About This?", explains the science behind the perfect competitive yawn: "It's all about maximum mouth aperture combined with optimal duration. Think of it as opera singing, but instead of hitting high notes, you're trying to look like a tired hippopotamus."

The sport consists of three main disciplines: Sprint Yawning (rapid-fire yawns under 30 seconds), Marathon Yawning (endurance events lasting up to four hours), and Synchronized Team Yawning (where groups of athletes attempt to yawn in perfect harmony). The scoring system takes into account factors such as mouth circumference, tear production, and the number of spectators infected by the competitor's yawn.

Training for competitive yawning is no joke – though it often looks like one. Elite yawners follow a strict regimen that includes:

Mouth Conditioning: Athletes stretch their jaw muscles by attempting to fit increasingly large objects into their mouths, starting with tennis balls and working their way up to small melons. World champion Marcus "The Maw" Thompson famously trained by trying to eat a watermelon whole, which earned him both respect and a lengthy dental bill.

Boredom Endurance: Competitors must build up their tolerance for mind-numbing activities. This typically involves watching paint dry, attending quarterly financial meetings, or sitting through extended family slideshows of vacation photos. The current world record holder, Agatha Burns, achieved her legendary status after surviving a 12-hour lecture on the history of beige paint.

Trigger Control: Advanced yawners learn to suppress their yawning reflex until the optimal moment, much like a ninja holding their breath. This requires watching countless videos of other people yawning without succumbing to the urge – a feat that has driven many promising athletes to switch to the less demanding sport of competitive sighing.

Equipment in competitive yawning is minimal but crucial. The official IFYA rulebook requires all athletes to wear the regulation "mouth sock" – a small mesh cover that prevents any accidental spittle from affecting other competitors. Some athletes also opt for optional gear like jaw supports and tear-catchers, though purists consider these to be crutches for the weak-willed.

The competitive scene has its share of controversy. The infamous "Sleeping Beauty Scandal" of 2019 rocked the sport when finalist Jimmy "The Sandman" Peters was discovered to have consumed twelve cups of chamomile tea before the championship match. While technically legal, it was considered poor sportsmanship and led to the creation of the "Natural Yawning" movement.

Strategy plays a crucial role in high-level competition. Veterans know that timing is everything. "You never want to peak too early," explains retired champion Maria Dozington. "I've seen rookies blow their best yawns in the warm-up room and end up looking like a confused goldfish during the actual competition."

The psychological warfare aspect of the sport cannot be understated. Elite yawners employ various tactics to throw off their opponents, such as making subtle sleeping noises or wearing extremely comfortable-looking pajamas during matches. Some competitors have been known to bring pillows as props, though this practice was banned after the "Great Nap-Off of 2020" when an entire tournament fell asleep mid-competition.

For those aspiring to enter the world of competitive yawning, coaches recommend starting with amateur night contests at local sleep clinics. Beginning yawners should focus on mastering the basics before attempting advanced techniques like the "Double-Wide Surprise" or the notorious "Sleeping Bear Revival."

The future of competitive yawning looks promising, with talks of Olympic inclusion for the 2032 games (though critics argue it might put spectators to sleep). The sport has even spawned several spin-off events, including speed napping and synchronized snoring.

As with any sport, competitive yawning requires dedication, perseverance, and an incredibly understanding family who won't mind you practicing at the dinner table. But for those who master it, the rewards are... yawn... excuse me... the rewards are truly worth the effort.

Remember the words of legendary coach Bob "Bedtime" Williams: "In competitive yawning, as in life, it's not about how wide you can open your mouth – it's about how many people you can make yawn with you." Words to sleep by, indeed.

(Note: If you found yourself yawning while reading this article, congratulations – you may have what it takes to be a champion. If not, well, there's always competitive blinking.)

Ending Thoughts - The Science of Taking Things Too Seriously

In the end, what are we to make of humanity's remarkable capacity to transform the ordinary into the extraordinary? After chronicling these diverse pursuits—from the metaphysical implications of belly button lint to the precise art of competitive eyebrow dancing—I find myself pondering the deeper significance of our collective tendency to overthink the unnecessary.

Consider the remarkable diversity of human obsession we've encountered. In the academic realm, we've seen scholars like Professor Marjorie Threadwell dedicate decades to understanding the profound implications of navel deposits, while Professor Eloise Brindle has revolutionized our understanding of ceiling fan communication. Their work, though perhaps unnecessary by conventional standards, speaks to humanity's endless capacity for finding complexity in simplicity.

The hobbyists we've met along the way prove equally fascinating. From Simon Lynch's determined journey into chopstick juggling to the underground world of subterranean yodelers, each practitioner has demonstrated that passion knows no bounds of practicality. Their dedication raises an essential question: Is it the activity itself that matters, or the simple act of pursuing mastery in whatever form it takes?

The equipment required for these pursuits tells its own story of human ingenuity. The "Importance Inflator 3000," the "Reality Check Station," and countless other specialized tools represent not just technological innovation, but our species' remarkable ability to create infrastructure around virtually any activity, no matter how obscure. Each carefully calibrated instrument and precisely engineered device serves as a testament to our determination to quantify and standardize even the most arbitrary of endeavors.

The emergence of distinct schools of thought within each discipline—be they the Meticulous Observers, Data-Driven Documentarians, or Theoretical Overthinkists—demonstrates how readily humans create complex social hierarchies and philosophical frameworks around any sustained activity. The heated debates between traditional lint collectors and modern practitioners, or between classical sock folders and avant-garde innovators, mirror the great academic disputes of our time, albeit on a slightly more peculiar scale.

Perhaps most telling is the economic ecosystem that inevitably develops around these pursuits. From specialized equipment manufacturers to professional competitions with substantial prize purses, we consistently find ways to monetize our obsessions, transforming personal passions into commercial enterprises. The fact that one can make a living as a professional eyebrow dancer or competitive pencil sharpener speaks volumes about our species' ability to create value from virtually anything.

What does this say about human nature? Are we, as some critics suggest, simply prone to overthinking? Or does our tendency to dive deep into the shallow end of human experience reveal something more profound about our need to find meaning and structure in a chaotic universe? When Dr. Fuzz-Worth examines a piece of lint under her custom-designed microscope, or when Simon Lynch perfects his chopstick juggling routine, are they not participating in the grand human tradition of seeking significance through specialized knowledge and skill?

As I conclude this chronicle of humanity's most overlooked achievements in overthinking, I'm struck by a simple truth: it's not the specific subject of study that matters, but rather the very human impulse to study anything and everything with unwarranted intensity. Whether we're analyzing the acoustic properties of belly buttons or documenting the migratory patterns of rubber ducks, we're really exploring our own need to understand, categorize, and master the world around us—no matter how unnecessary that mastery might be.

In the end, perhaps that's the real significance of these seemingly insignificant pursuits. They remind us that human curiosity and dedication know no bounds, that meaning can be found (or created) in the most unlikely places, and that sometimes the most profound insights come from studying the utterly ordinary with extraordinary attention.

As I prepare to leave my office at the International Institute of Improbable Research to retire on the beach in Newscastle, I glance at the custom-designed lint microscope on my desk and the carefully cataloged collection of rubber ducks migrating across my bookshelf. I can't help but smile, knowing that somewhere out there, someone is preparing to take something simple far too seriously—and in doing so, they're participating in one of humanity's most peculiar and endearing traditions.

After all, isn't the ability to find complexity in simplicity, to create meaning where none existed before, one of our species' most remarkable traits? And if that means spending decades studying the metaphysical implications of belly button lint or the secret language of ceiling fans, well, perhaps that's exactly what makes us human.

Appendice – A

Research Notes from the Reject Pile: A Peer-Reviewed Collection of Misfit Studies

Every book has its cutting room floor, littered with perfectly good stories that, for one reason or another, refused to play nicely with the others. Like a researcher who spends three years studying the acoustic properties of cheese only to discover their findings are too niche even for the Journal of Improbable Research, sometimes you have to know when to let go.

These are the stories that made me grin, raised my eyebrows, or sent me down three-day research rabbit holes, but ultimately demanded their own space. They're not outcasts or rejects—think of them more as academic free agents, too independent to be bound by traditional chapter constraints. So consider this section a controlled experiment in narrative liberation, where each story can finally do what it does best: be absolutely, unapologetically itself.

Dr. Henri Penuer

15th of January. 2025

Ashton Croft, Is-Still-Broke, England

Extreme Sock Folding

In the pristine world of competitive sock folding, where victories are measured in millimeters and careers can be unraveled by a single misaligned heel, the pursuit of the perfect pair has evolved into an art form rivaling traditional Japanese origami. Dr. Victoria Foldsworth, director of the International Sock Folding Institute (ISFI), has spent two decades documenting what she terms "the textile transformation revolution."

The taxonomy of competitive sock folding reveals three distinct schools: the Traditional Bundlers (Sockus compactus), the Military-Precision Folders (Sockus militaris), and the avant-garde Sculptural Expressionists (Sockus artistica). Each group maintains its own techniques, traditions, and deeply held beliefs about the true nature of sock harmony.

Consider the case of James "Swift Hands" Martinez, twelve-time world champion in the Speed Folding Division. "People think it's just about matching pairs," he explains, demonstrating his signature "Thunder Clap" technique on a pristine set of merino wool socks. "But at this level, you're really conducting a symphony of cotton and elastane."

The equipment requirements for elite folding have evolved dramatically. The Basic Competition Kit, as mandated by ISFI regulations, includes calibrated folding boards, humidity monitors, and what practitioners call a "rescue kit" – specialized tools for recovering stretched elastic. Advanced competitors often add controversial equipment like the "Static Eliminator 3000" and temperature-controlled storage cases.

Field research has revealed fascinating regional variations in technique. The Japanese school emphasizes minimal compression marks, while German competitors focus on geometric precision through their patented "Quadrat-Falten" method. Meanwhile, the emerging Korean style combines elements of both, creating what experts call a "harmonious fusion of form and function."

Dr. Heinrich von Sockenheim, author of "The Perfect Fold: Psychology of Competitive Sock Architecture," has identified distinct personality types among competitors. "The 'Precision Folders' approach each sock like a surgeon," he notes, "while the 'Intuitive Artists' claim they can feel the natural folding points in the fabric."

The economic implications of competitive folding have not gone unnoticed. The professional circuit, sponsored by leading sock manufacturers, offers substantial prizes. "Last year's Grand Prix winner took home $30,000 and a lifetime supply of premium compression socks," reveals Timothy Elastic, CEO of Elite Hosiery International.

Training regimens for competitive folders border on monastic dedication. The legendary "Thousand Pairs" exercise requires aspirants to fold one hundred pairs daily for ten days, achieving identical results with each fold. "It's not about the socks," explains Master Trainer Yuki Tanaka. "It's about finding the perfect fold within yourself."

Recent technological developments have sparked intense debate within the community. The introduction of automated folding assistance devices has traditionalists in an uproar. "If you need more than your hands and your heart, you're in the wrong sport," argues Maria Doblez, holder of the current speed-folding record.

For now, the elite world of competitive sock folding continues to evolve, pushing the boundaries of human precision and patience. As James Martinez likes to say while arranging his competition-grade ankle socks, "In life, as in folding, true perfection lies not in the final form, but in the journey to achieve it."

Mastering the Art of Competitive Kazoo Playing

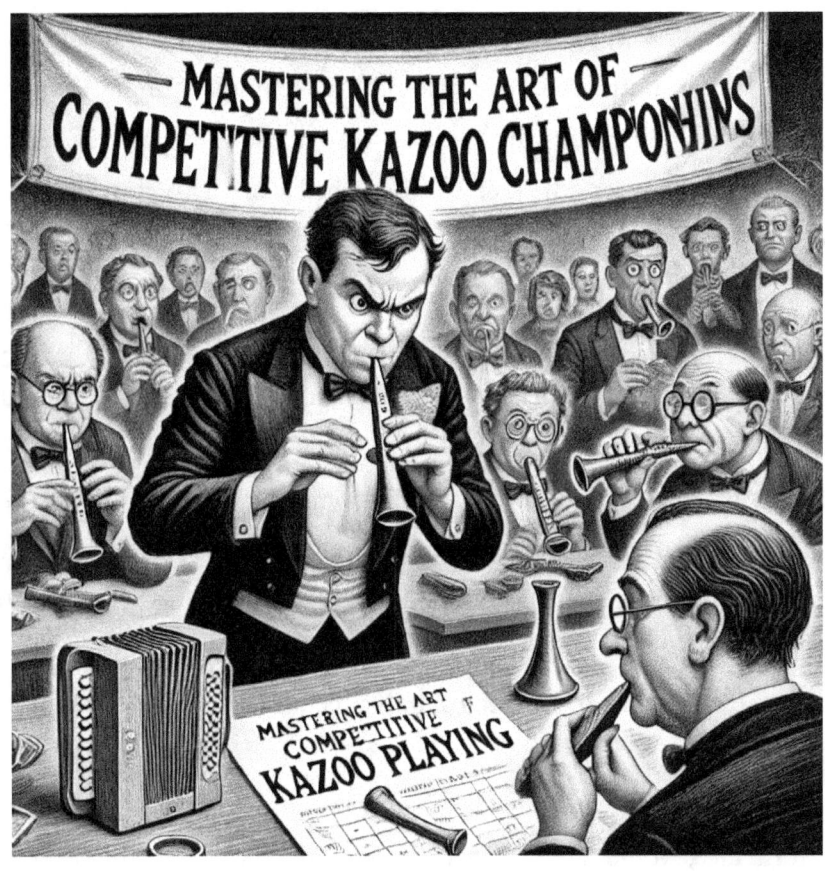

In the dimly lit practice rooms of the International Kazoo Federation (IKF), where plastic instruments gleamed like precious metals and breathing exercises echoed through soundproofed walls, Eleanor "The Buzzer" Martinez had mastered the subtle art of competitive kazooing.

Her fifteen-year career as a professional kazoo athlete had prepared her for precisely this moment: the perfect execution of what enthusiasts called "The Fibonacci Sequence" - a series of ascending hums that could bring audiences to tears.

"The kazoo isn't just an instrument," Eleanor would later explain to her trophy collection. "It's an extension of the soul, filtered through a small plastic tube."

Dmitri Kazookov, three-time World Kazoo Championship finalist and pioneer of the controversial "Double-Breath Technique," understood the competitive kazoo circuit with the intensity of a quantum physicist studying parallel universes. His lucky kazoo - shellacked with clear nail polish and never washed - wasn't merely an instrument, but a battle-tested weapon of mass distraction.

"Traditional musicians have nothing on competitive kazoo players," Dmitri would eventually tell his meditation guru. "This is where real musical warfare happens - one buzz-off at a time."

Their paths crossed in the warm-up room at the Annual Grand Prix of Kazoo, a neutral territory where the sophisticated dance of pre-competition intimidation reached its peak. Eleanor, practicing her signature "Triple Tremolo Twist" with the intensity of a surgeon performing heart surgery, executed a perfect pitch slide - a technique she'd spent decades perfecting.

Her metronome, which she'd named "Tick" and consulted before every performance, would later witness her detailed analysis: "In the complex ecosystem of competitive kazoo playing, the warm-up room represents both sanctuary and psychological battleground. One must appear simultaneously focused and relaxed, masterful yet approachable, intense yet zen-like."

Dmitri's pre-performance ritual, visible from across the practice hall, was a masterpiece of methodical preparation. Each breathing exercise - deliberate, measured, and completely incomprehensible to the uninitiated - contributed to what he called his "sonic preparation framework."

"The competitive kazoo environment," Dmitri would later note in his performance diary, "operates on a complex system of respiratory warfare. The sound of warming up often intimidates more than the performance itself."

Eleanor's collection of kazoos, arranged in a chromatic scale on her custom-built display case, contained instruments from every major plastic manufacturer. "Kazoo selection," she would explain during mandatory post-competition interviews, "is less about the instrument and more about the psychological advantage of having more kazoos than your opponents."

Their shared mastery of the art of competitive kazooing had earned them an unspoken mutual respect. Eleanor's ability to maintain perfect pitch while performing her signature "Reverse Butterfly Pattern" complemented Dmitri's groundbreaking work in experimental kazoo harmonics.

"In the delicate ballet of competitive kazoo mastery," Eleanor would later confide to her trophy collection during their 3:15 PM polishing session, "the key lies not in just making noise, but in elevating noise into an art form that questions the very foundations of what we consider music."

Competitive Rubber Band Archery (Draft for submission)

The rubber band on Dr. Julio Ramirez's desk had always been there, coiled like a patient serpent around his collection of blue ballpoint pens. But for Julio, it wasn't just an office supply—it was his destiny. And destinies, as any tenured professor would tell you, require peer-reviewed documentation.

"What exactly are you measuring?" his colleague, Dr. Patricia Murray, asked one afternoon, watching him calibrate his newly invented Elastic Tension Quantification Device (a modified kitchen scale).

"Not measuring, Pat," Julio replied, adjusting his prescription safety goggles with NASA-grade precision. "I'm documenting the dialectical relationship between potential and kinetic energy in office-grade elastic projectiles." He paused to log another data point. "Some people call it shooting rubber bands."

Patricia retreated to her office, leaving Julio to his elastic experiments. He remained undaunted. After all, he'd already revolutionized the field of rubber band dynamics with his groundbreaking taxonomy of elastic personalities:

The thin, pale ones from the mail room—classified as "Nervous Novices" in his research—displayed inconsistent trajectory patterns and a tendency toward catastrophic structural failure. The medium-width bands—"Steady Performers"—offered reliable but uninspiring ballistic performance, suitable primarily for binding together rejected grant proposals. But the thick, amber-colored specimens—"Elite Snappers"—these were the ones that achieved what he called "perfect aerodynamic poetry."

Julio documented all these findings in his magnum opus, "Elastic Trajectories: A Comprehensive Study of Rubber Band Ballistics (Volume 1 of 7)." The real breakthrough came during a particularly tedious faculty meeting when he discovered that rubber bands exhibited distinct behavioral patterns based on their storage environments. Bands kept in direct sunlight developed what he termed "brittle personality disorder," while those stored in his climate-controlled desk drawer maintained optimal elasticity coefficients.

"Environmental adaptation," he muttered, frantically recording his observations while his colleagues discussed such trivial matters as tenure and parking privileges.

His research attracted inevitable attention. "Are you... constructing some sort of rubber band firing range in your office?" Dean Thompson inquired one morning, examining the elaborate target system Julio had engineered from color-coded file folders and recycled academic journals.

"Not a firing range, Dean Thompson," Julio corrected, demonstrating his patented "Ramirez Trajectory Technique." "This is a state-of-the-art elastic projectile research facility." The dean watched in silence as Julio executed a perfect parabolic arc, landing a size-33 band precisely in his pencil holder from a distance of 3.7 meters.

"Fascinating," the dean murmured, backing slowly toward the door.

The custodial staff proved less enthusiastic about his research, particularly after discovering rubber bands in the ceiling tiles, behind the water cooler, and somehow inside the sealed coffee maker. Julio simply added these findings to his ongoing study titled "Migration Patterns of Feral Elastic Bands in Closed Office Ecosystems."

Sandra from Accounting remained his harshest critic. "Isn't this just playing with rubber bands?" she asked during one of his mandatory demonstration sessions.

Julio adjusted his safety goggles with grave solemnity. "Sandra," he replied, "that's like saying Marie Curie was just playing with glowing rocks."

As his research expanded, Julio began correlating band behavior with atmospheric conditions. Humid days produced what he termed "suboptimal snap velocity," while dry, crisp mornings yielded perfect elastic performance. His resulting "Ramirez Scale of Elastic Optimality" now covered an entire wall of his office, much to the concern of the building's structural engineer.

Patricia now takes the long way to the break room, just to be safe. But for Julio, each day brings new discoveries in the field of elastic projectiles. And if some fail to appreciate the gravity of his research—well, as he often reminds his increasingly concerned colleagues, "In the grand rubber band of life, we're all just waiting for the right moment to snap."

Afterword

If you would like to to read more about the exploits of the author – follow him at froginasock.substack.com where he likes to hang out.   Or you can send an email to inquiries @twohungrybowlers.com.

Oh.

and support independent bookstores especially local ones if you can.